Doolies

Nancy Thurman

EPIC
Press

Doolies
Freshmen: Book #3

Written by Nancy Thurman

Copyright © 2017 by Abdo Consulting Group, Inc.

Published by EPIC Press™
PO Box 398166
Minneapolis, MN 55439

Cover design by Kali VanZuilen
Images for cover art obtained from iStockPhoto.com
Edited by Kirsten Rue

Library of Congress Cataloging-in-Publication Data

Names: Thurman, Nancy, author.
Title: Doolies / by Nancy Thurman.
Description: Minneapolis, MN : EPIC Press, [2017] | Series: Freshmen
Summary: Nash Kaplan is straddling two worlds: one where he can sleep until noon, eat chips,
    and instant message his friends; and another of pre-dawn wake-ups, no internet or cell
    phones, and standing at attention. Over 1,000 kids come to the United States Air Force
    Academy to begin their college experience, and many drop out before they complete their
    freshman year, their Doolie year. Nash must decide which world he wants, before the choice
    is made for him.
Identifiers: LCCN 2016931771 | ISBN 9781680763461 (lib. bdg.) |
    ISBN 9781680763324 (ebook)
Subjects: LCSH: College students—Fiction. | Identity—Fiction. | Interpersonal relations—
    Fiction. | Young adult fiction.
Classification: DDC [Fic]—dc23
LC record available at http://lccn.loc.gov/2016931771

EPICPRESS.COM

*To my boys, Grayson and Jack,
and to my grandparents, Dave and Linda.
Thank you.*

PROLOGUE

"You ready to leave for college, Nash? I bet your mom isn't ready to let you go."

Mr. Parsons shook Nash's hand hard as he patted him on the shoulder. Without waiting for Nash to answer, Mr. Parsons continued, "Did you know I served in Desert Storm? Lived in a tent with fifty other guys. Showered once a week. But every month we'd get these giant crab legs in the mess hall . . . I don't know where they found these crabs, but their legs were as big as your arm . . . "

Nash wasn't listening. Ever since he was accepted to the Air Force Academy, every person in

Clarksville had a war story to tell him. He was over it and he hadn't even started yet. He just wanted to get there already. After filling out the application and submitting the essays, letters of recommendation, transcripts, and test scores, he had to get an endorsement from one of his state representatives. With all the hoops to jump through, it was almost like the Academy was trying to get rid of folks before they were even accepted. But Nash jumped through them all, and he received his welcome letter three months ago. He had been counting down the days ever since.

Nash knew his mom was having a hard time with him going to school so far away from home. But he also knew she was proud of him. Mason was not ready, though. Nash knew his little brother was bummed. "You could stay here, live at home for awhile, and then we could go off to college together when I graduate in a couple years. I don't know why you're being such a jerk about this." Mason punched him in the arm—hard—when

Nash laughed at his suggestion. Nash didn't feel like a jerk. He felt like he was about to explode if he didn't see what else was out there.

It had only been the three of them—Nash, Mason, and their mom—for so many years that Mason was taking Nash's departure harder than Nash expected. They had only grown closer since the boys' father died when Nash was twelve and Mason was nine. Soon, it would only be Mom and Mason.

Nash tugged at the too-tight tie around his neck as he stood outside the church where his cousin Jimmy had just married his high school girlfriend. Just then, Jimmy and his new bride pushed through the chapel doors and ran down the sidewalk through the birdseed being tossed in the air.

Nash envied Jimmy. He'd known what he wanted to do with his life when he was ten. He was going to finish Clarksville High, marry his girl, and take over his dad's refrigerator business—in that order. And so far, he was moving along according to plan. Nash's jealousy wasn't dark though. He and his cousin were the same age; they had grown up playing on the hay bales at Uncle Frank's farm since they were in diapers. Nash loved Jimmy, and was happy to see his life working out. He just wanted his to work out, too, and he wanted not to have to figure out what the plan was anymore. Maybe the Academy was the answer.

Nash waved at Jimmy as the happy couple jumped into a borrowed Cadillac. "See you later, cuz!" Nash yelled after him, as the car pulled away from the curb.

Nash's mom came up beside him and put her arm around his waist. Her head barely came up to his shoulders now. Nash slung his arm around her. "Well, momma," he said. She grinned every time he called her "momma" mostly because he said it like he was Elvis Presley, humming the *mmm* at the beginning. "It's time to head over to the reception hall, I guess."

His mom looked up at him with watery eyes,

and gave his waist a squeeze. "Why don't you take off and say goodbye to your friends . . . Grandma and Grandpa will see you in the morning before you get on the plane, and you know I won't get a wink's sleep until I lay eyes on you tonight. Maybe check in with Mason though," she nodded toward Nash's brother. He was leaning against a tree staring off into nothing. "He's going to miss you so much."

"Just him, momma?" he Elvis-ed again.

She looked up at him, and then a tear fell. "You'll be back," she said.

"Yep. November's going to be here before you know it."

CHAPTER

1

This is bullshit. Bullshit. Bullshit. Bullshit. The word echoed through Nash's brain as the military training instructor yelled just inches from his face.

The man stood eye-level with Nash, so that would make him about six feet. Nash didn't know what his face looked like yet, because he was told to "CAGE YOUR EYES, AND STOP EYEBALLING ME!" Nash quickly learned not to look directly into it—the face—er, the instructor's face. The orders kept thundering in at him:

"GET YOUR HEELS TOGETHER, BASIC!"

That was Nash's new name: Basic.

"DON'T LOOK DOWN!"

"DON'T YOU KNOW WHERE YOUR FEET ARE WITHOUT LOOKING?" another one launched in on him, apparently having a good time this Sunday morning yelling in people's faces.

"GET YOUR EYES FORWARD AND YOUR HEELS TOGETHER, BASIC!" another one joined in.

"DON'T YOU EYEBALL ME, BASIC. EYES FORWARD! HEELS TOGETHER!"

Don't look at them, Nash! Now, he was talking to himself. Not an hour into the first day, and Nash was ready to lose his mind.

"CUP YOUR HANDS, BASIC!" Another member of the basic training cadre, made up of military training instructors and Academy upper-classmen, had joined in on the event: Nash Bash 2016. Nash could feel the sweat make a beeline down his back, and he was losing his grip on the giant duffle bag his mom had bought him as a going-away-to-college present. When he had tried to put it down, he was greeted with another onslaught of yelling for failing to ask permission to "ground his gear."

"STAND AT ATTENTION!" from a fourth. How many could they spare? Weren't there any other basics around that needed attention? And how was Nash supposed to tell if his heels were together if he wasn't allowed to look? And why all the yelling? He could hear them just fine in a normal tone. The instructor was totally invading his personal space, inches away from his nose, even. But maybe he was so close because there was so much yelling going on *everywhere*, so in order for this guy to be clear about exactly who he was yelling at, he felt he needed to get right up close.

In reality, the Smokey the Bear hat the instructor wore provided at least a three-inch buffer zone between Nash's nose and the instructor's nose. But that buffer zone felt like centimeters rather than inches, and that hat didn't do much to keep the volume down. The man had a booming voice that already cut through Nash's eardrums and drilled into his brain to the place where all Nash's good memories were stored. That voice kicked all those good memories right in the balls.

Nash was yelled at before he'd even stepped off the large blue school bus that had brought him from the visitor's center to "The Hill," where the Academy was situated.

The Hill was actually a valley surrounded by mountains and Colorado sky. If he had time, Nash would be awestruck by the beauty of this amazing place, and how unlike Clarksville it was. Where Clarksville was flat and full of cornfields, Colorado was elevated with jutting rock faces and tree-covered mountaintops. In Clarksville, Nash imagined he could see the curvature of the Earth, as miles upon miles of sky were visible over all the farmland and open prairies. Not so in Colorado. The sky was in competition with, well, everything else. But Nash didn't notice any of this at that moment.

"GET OVER HERE AND GET IN LINE!"

Who should he listen to now? He was surrounded by people yelling at him to get his feet together, cup his hands, cage his eyes (How could he do that, anyway? Did they expect him to remove his eyes from his head and lock them up? Nash knew the military had a reputation for doing crazy things, but that was crossing the line, right?) *Please, don't let them expect me to gouge out my eyes*, Nash said a silent prayer.

"CAN YOU HEAR ME, BASIC? GET OVER HERE NOW!"

Behind Smokey, who was still snarling about Nash getting his heels together, there was a fifth yeller. But this one didn't have a special hat. And he didn't have Smokey's voice either. This voice had the shrillness of a screaming bird protecting his food supply, or a piglet caught in a barbed wire fence. Unbearable. Nash wanted to make it stop. He made a move toward that voice. But as Nash hurriedly stepped forward, his shoulder brushed against Smokey who was inches away and yelling into his left eye.

"ARE YOU TRYING TO ASSAULT ME, BASIC? ARE YOU TRYING TO CHARGE ME?" Smokey snarled.

Nash almost laughed at the absurdity of the situation. *Did this guy really just say that?* Nash just spent what felt like two years being yelled at by more people than he could keep straight, and this guy actually had the nerve to accuse him of assault? This was bullshit. And all the YouTube videos he watched in preparation for this very day were bullshit, too. They didn't truly capture the spit flying all over the place, or the weight of his duffle bag growing heavier and heavier as he stood there unable to move his eyeballs freely, or exactly how fucking difficult it was to keep his damn heels together without looking down.

Before Nash could open his mouth to answer,

Smokey bellowed, "GET OUT OF MY SIGHT, BASIC. GET OVER THERE!" The instructor pointed in the direction of the squealing piglet, and Nash took off running. He actually breathed a sigh of relief as he moved away from one uncomfortable situation into another one. He was only twenty-seven minutes into day one.

CHAPTER 2

The rest of the morning really didn't get better. Between periods of time where Smokey and the mentally deranged upperclassmen seemed to flock to Nash's side to yell at him, Nash was supposed to be studying his blue book. The blue book was small enough that Nash could store it in his pants pocket as he ran from "OVER HERE" to "OVER THERE." And whenever he arrived "HERE" or "THERE," he was taught to dig the book out immediately. His lesson went like this:

"HERE'S YOUR CONTRAILS, BASIC. YOU NEED TO KNOW EVERYTHING IN IT. START STUDYING!" An upperclassman with an unnaturally neat bun—like the robot in *Terminator 3: Rise of the Machines*—handed him a blue book. She almost wasn't yelling. Almost.

"Right now?" Silly Nash. Questions are for upperclassmen, not basics.

Before Neat Bun could answer him, Smokey came from somewhere behind Nash's peripheral vision and yelled, "THAT'S NOT ONE OF THE SEVEN BASIC RESPONSES, BASIC! WHAT ARE THE SEVEN BASIC RESPONSES?" Without pausing a half-second for a response, Smokey continued, "YOU DON'T KNOW THE SEVEN BASIC RESPONSES BECAUSE YOU'RE NOT STUDYING YOUR CONTRAILS! OPEN YOUR CONTRAILS AND STUDY, BASIC!"

After that verbal kick to his eardrums, Nash learned to study his blue book. And after another loud lesson about taking up too much space, he learned to keep the book three inches from his face, which really made studying easier. It felt *totally* natural to read with the words *inches* from his eye sockets. If Nash could have rolled his eyes with certainty that it wouldn't attract attention, he would. Instead, he thought, *This is bullshit.*

Nash thought about all the preparation it took to get here, to Colorado, to the Air Force Academy, to this hallway where skinny-ass punks in blue Smurf shirts and pants were screaming at him. Was this why he signed up to take all those advanced-placement math courses when everyone else was sailing through Algebra? Was this why he joined the Chemistry Club and worked his ass off to understand algorithms for some science competition while his buddies went camping and fishing every weekend? Was this why he scrimped and saved every penny he could to take flying lessons instead of getting a new truck? Shit. He hoped not. He hoped there was more in store for him than getting yelled at.

The basics had been herded, like human cattle, inside what the cadets called Fairchild Hall. Everything looked the same to Nash, who had finally learned to cage his eyes. Honestly, if someone blindfolded him and moved him three feet away, he would be lost—unable to find his way back to where he came from—he couldn't tell the difference between any hallway or any building.

Not able to concentrate on the blue book, Nash tried to stretch out his side eye muscles without turning his head. He discovered he could start seeing someone before they came directly even with his shoulders. Satisfied that he had stretched his side eye as far as it would go for now, Nash turned his concentration back to memorizing the information in the blue book.

The hallway was strangely quiet with the exception of a page turned, a cough here or there, and the sucking sound of a basic drinking from his CamelBak, a water backpack that each of them had been issued that morning. They were ordered to fill it up and "HYDRATE"—like every twenty minutes.

Nash had actually gotten used to the yelling. It

only took three hours, but he no longer vibrated with people hollering at the same time. As long as it wasn't Smokey. It's not that Nash had never been yelled at before. He had played sports, and the coaches at Clarksville High were not always patient teachers, but they didn't circle him like a swarm of pissed-off piranhas.

"When are you done, today?" an upperclassman chatted up Neat Bun who was leaning against the wall, right in Nash's field of view. The upperclassmen and instructors were the only people allowed to carry on normal conversations. They were the only people allowed to lean, too. Nash already missed talking to people . . . and leaning. He missed moving his eyeballs freely. He missed having space between his heels.

"I'm done in an hour. I've been on since oh-six hundred." Her voice was matter-of-fact, not really inviting the upperclassman to continue.

Not gonna happen, dude, Nash thought. He

even missed girls rejecting him. This place was destroying his psyche.

"I'm here until twenty-one hundred. Gotta put the smacks to bed." He chuckled. Some upperclassmen called the freshmen *smacks* as a way to make fun of them. The name represented the sound of shit hitting the wall: *Smack!*

"Don't call them that. I hated that," Neat Bun asserted. Then she continued, "They'll be so happy to go to sleep tonight. Remember?" she asked, taking a walk down memory lane about this time in life that was making Nash rethink every piece of paper he signed to get here.

Suddenly, they both straightened off the wall and before Nash could ensure his eyes weren't looking around willy-nilly, Smokey came into view and bellowed. "GET YOUR FACE IN YOUR CONTRAILS!"

Nash's shoulders jumped back a little and his arm automatically snapped up straighter, elbow out, parallel to the ground. Smokey started toward him, and he braced himself for this next round of verbal punches, but the instructor walked right past Nash to the person standing behind him—he had no idea who the poor sucker was, but he was glad it wasn't him this time.

Smokey continued to question the basic, but quietly, which was somehow more terrifying than yelling. "Do you know the mission of the Academy, Basic?" Smokey hissed. Nash's neck hairs stood at attention.

"N-no, sir." The basic responded in a tiny voice that trembled like he was going to burst into tears right there in Fairchild Hall.

Don't do it, dude. Nash sent him mental motivation. *Hang in there, Guy-I-Can't-See. Just put your face in the book.*

Smokey rolled out question after question, not waiting for the basic to stammer out any answers. "You don't know the mission of the Air Force Academy? Why not? How can you not know the mission of the Air Force Academy? Aren't you trying to become a cadet at the Academy?"

"Yes, I want to be a ca—"

"IS THAT ONE OF THE SEVEN BASIC RESPONSES, BASIC?" Smokey erupted, and Nash physically jerked at the unexpected explosion.

"No, sir—I-I-I don't know the res—" The basic's stammer worsened.

"IS THAT ONE OF THE SEVEN BASIC RESPONSES, BASIC?" No one dared move within the hallway.

"No, sir." The basic's voice quavered.

"IF YOU DON'T KNOW THE SEVEN BASIC RESPONSES AND YOU DON'T KNOW THE MISSION OF THE AIR FORCE ACADEMY, I SHOULDN'T SEE YOU LOOKING ANYWHERE BUT IN YOUR CONTRAILS!"

Nash could hear everyone in the hallway straightening up their arms and getting their eyes glued to the pages of the blue book. He quickly turned to the page with the Academy's mission statement. Intuitively, he knew every other basic in the hallway was doing the same as he heard the frantic flipping of paper.

Smokey came into Nash's peripheral vision, walking past him toward Neat Bun and her companion. He couldn't hear what Smokey said to them next, but after he was finished, they both hurried off in different directions with a quick, "Yes, sir!"

Slowly, Smokey turned back to survey the basics lined up along the hallways of Fairchild Hall. If Neat Bun was one of the machines from *Terminator 3*, then Smokey was the Terminator himself. He was one scary sonofabitch. And the sniffles of the basic behind Nash were evidence of that.

———

"STOW YOUR CONTRAILS. IT'S TIME FOR LUNCH," one of the upperclassmen yelled, and all the basics within earshot (which was probably every single one in Colorado) hastily put away their blue books. Lunchtime. As if on cue, Nash's stomach growled. As the basics formed a line, some of the upperclassmen handed them boxed lunches—literally lunches in white gift boxes.

Nash thought, *Holy Shit! Is this how I'm going to eat for the next six weeks? I can't survive on a turkey sandwich and some orange slices. I'm going to starve to death.* When he opened the box, there was a turkey sandwich with American cheese, tightly wrapped in Saran Wrap. He also had a bag of Cool Ranch Doritos (Nash's favorite), some carrot and celery sticks, an apple, a banana, and a brownie, secured in the Fort Knox of Saran Wrap again. Nash was disappointed not to receive a juice box like other kids at summer camp, but he remembered the ever-present water backpack that was steadily leaking down his back, leaving a wet imprint through his vintage Rolling Stones t-shirt.

Not too bad, Nash thought, as he dug into the sandwich and bag of chips.

"HURRY UP AND STUFF YOUR FACES. LUNCH ENDS IN FIVE MINUTES!"

Five minutes wasn't the leisurely dining experience Nash had hoped for, but they were allowed to pop a squat on the polished marble of the hallway. It felt good to sit down, to uncage the eyeballs, and finally get some visual bearings of the place.

Elevators to the left, okay. So the building has multiple floors, he guessed. *Good to know.* There appeared to be some sort of lobby past the elevators with cream-colored leather chairs, tables, and Persian rugs. It looked comfortable, welcoming. A resting place for busy cadets going from class to class. It looked like a normal college. Again, Nash felt his hope restored. Maybe this place wasn't going to be the biggest mistake he'd ever made.

To his right, there was a . . . store? Like a real-life college bookstore with snacks and t-shirts, Monster drinks, and iPhone chargers. He could see it all through the windows. And there were other cadets in there. Their backpacks slung over their shoulders, their uniforms crisp. They were smiling. One of them walked past the basics all noshing on their sandwiches with their backs against the plain walls, and he winked at Nash. He actually fucking winked, like sitting with your back against these walls, getting yelled at by shrill jerks was some secret ritual, and he was letting Nash in on the joke.

Okay, okay. I can do this. I can make it through these six shitty weeks. And I can make it through this freshman year, this Doolie year, Nash was talking to himself again, but this time trying to psyche himself up. But before he could carry the conversation further, lunch was over.

"GET UP! CLEAN UP YOUR AREA. I DON'T WANT TO SEE ONE SINGLE PIECE

OF TRASH ON MY FLOOR. I DON'T WANT
ONE SLIVER OF POTATO CHIP OR ONE
CUPCAKE CRUMB. AND YOU BETTER
HAVE ENJOYED THIS LUNCH TODAY,
BASICS. YOU WERE SPOILED TODAY.
DON'T GET USED TO IT." Smokey's voice
filled every crevice of Nash's happy place—once
again kicking everything in the balls.

It was time for haircuts. Every male had to get his head shaved, and every female had to make sure her hair was in a bun if it was long enough to touch her shoulders. Nash stood in formation, a sardine neatly lined up in an invisible can, as he waited with the other male basics outside of the Academy's barbershop. Every few minutes another chair opened up, and another head of hair cascaded to the floor. The women and men who were shaving heads stood amidst piles of it, and it kept growing at their feet. When it was Nash's turn, he sat in the chair and met his own eyes in the mirror. He almost felt relief at seeing a friendly face, except his face didn't look that friendly. His eyes, usually a lively sky blue, appeared gray in the mirror. His eyebrows were scrunched toward the middle of his forehead, and his lips were little more than a thin, tense line on his face. He felt like this was it for some reason—like he couldn't turn back once the hair came off. When his brown locks hit the floor, he would no longer be whomever he was in Clarksville. Who would he be? Nash knew the haircuts were coming, but he hadn't anticipated it being so emotional. He knew it was ridiculous. It was only hair, right?

He had certainly had his head shaved before, lots of times. Every summer Nash's dad would have him drag a chair from the kitchen table out to the garage. He would wrap a towel around Nash's shoulders, get out the clippers, and slowly, carefully shave off strips of hair starting from the sides and moving toward the top until he had made a Mohawk. Then he would send Nash inside to find his mom and ask if he could keep his hair that way. She would pretend to be out-raged, and order him back outside to get a proper buzz cut, but Nash knew she was only playing along. His kid-self loved all of it. He loved the feel of his dad's big, rough hands trying to be gentle with the clippers, he loved it when his dad would sing along to Neil Diamond's "Sweet Caroline" when it came on the radio, he loved it when his dad would turn the garden hose on Nash and his brother and would chase them around the backyard trying to rinse the hair off.

But he hadn't had his head completely shaved since his dad died. With his monthly trim at Clip 'N Save, he had grown proud of his hair. He took a lot of time getting it to look just right every morning. Mason would make fun of him because he took twice as long as him to get ready. And, yes, maybe he did like his hair to look nice. So what? Did that make him a bad person?

There was chatter and even some laughter in the barbershop as the men and women tried to put the basics at ease. They weren't part of the cadre chosen to train the basics and guide them through the rigors of basic training. They were just regular folks, with the simple job of cutting hair. They treated the basics like ordinary customers, so for those few minutes, Nash almost felt like a real person again. There was a television set on in the corner and the Nuggets were playing the Pacers in Indiana. The perfect storm of thinking about his last buzz cut, the Pacers on the tube, and being talked to like a normal human being almost had the tears falling over Nash's eyelids. He looked up to the corner of the barbershop's ceiling, willing the tears to get back in there.

The barber was finished in less than five minutes. "That does it." The man removed the cape from around Nash's neck and noticed Nash's eyes watering. "Did you get hair in your eyes? There's so much floating around here . . . before I head home tonight, my wife will turn the hose on me to get rid of all this stuff. This day is one of the hairiest . . . "

The barber kept talking, giving Nash time to collect himself and giving him an excuse for the tears threatening to overtake him.

"Yeah, I got something in my eye."

"Let me get you a fresh towel. Hold on." The barber left for a few seconds and came back with a clean blue towel. Everything in this place was blue. Nash took it with a smile and began wiping at his eyes, pretending to be wiping the hairs away.

"Good luck. Hang in there," the barber said, giving Nash a knowing smile and turning away as he called for the next basic.

———————

After several more hours of running over here and waiting over there, filling in administrative forms, getting his military identification card (in his picture he looked like a hairless farm cat), talking to a doctor about his chicken pox experience of 2004, getting jabbed with some vaccinations he didn't know he needed, and eating dinner, it was finally time to head to the dorms and sleep. Nash couldn't wait to lay his head down anywhere and call this day over.

After running across the campus to the sleeping quarters, Nash found himself standing at attention in the hallway outside his dorm room. The bed was so close, but still so far away.

An upperclassman was walking down the hallway giving instructions, "YOU'RE GOING TO GO INTO YOUR ROOMS, MAKE UP YOUR BEDS, PERFORM YOUR HYGIENE, AND GET TO SLEEP—YOU HAVE SEVEN MINUTES. GET TO IT!"

Perform your hygiene? Do people really talk like that? Nash thought. Then, as if released from a holding pen, every basic in the dorm began scrambling around, some jumping into their rooms to begin making up their beds, others running toward the community bathroom situated in the middle of the hallway. Nash and his roommate collided at the doorframe of their room as they both tried to get through it at the same time. It would have been hilarious if Nash wasn't so tired and over this day.

The room was bleak, to put a positive spin on it. It was made of cinder blocks painted a pale bluish grey, like the color of rain clouds. Against one wall was a metal-framed bunk bed. Nash imagined this was the same style found in most prison systems. Each bunk had a plastic mattress like he used to have before he learned to control his bladder when he was six. Each bunk also had sheets with "Property of US Government" stenciled on them, a plastic-covered pillow, and a GI blanket like Nash had seen in every military movie since military movies existed. Everything was tossed in a haphazard pile on the bottom bunk.

"Well, this isn't exactly the Four Seasons."

Nash's bunkmate broke the silence first. "Holy shit, look at this place. It's like the yelling and the running, and the fuckin' eyeball bullshit weren't enough to make you want to quit. Then they put our asses in this monochromatic shithole for four years."

"Either that or they're trying to make us kill ourselves." Nash replied, not filtering any of the thoughts that were inside his head.

"Whoa! That went dark fast, dude. You're not going to be one of those roommates I have to watch out for, are you? I mean, am I going to come back to the room one day and find that you've covered all the walls with black garbage bags, and you're listening to Five Finger Death Punch on an endless loop?"

The ridiculousness of the vision made Nash laugh out loud. "No Five Finger Death Punch or garbage bags, I promise."

"Good. I'm Jake Nichols," Jake said as he held out his hand and Nash shook it.

"Nash Kaplan."

As they made up their bunks, Nash taking the top bunk after Jake joked that he was afraid of heights, the two continued to talk.

"So, what's your story, Nash?"

"What do you mean?" Nash asked, too tired to carry on a conversation.

"I mean, like, where are you from? How did you end up at the Academy? You know, the regular shit people are supposed to ask. Fuck, don't tell me you're suicidal *and* socially awkward." Jake chuckled and threw the GI blanket up to Nash on the top bunk.

Nash laughed at Jake's joke and replied, "Nope, I'm not. But I *am* from Indiana. You?"

"I'm a brat. Grew up military, so I don't really have one place I consider home. I'm an only child, so that will be my excuse for anything you don't like . . . I have a dog named Tater, and my parents are still married and live in Houston. Your turn."

Nash paused. Normally, he wouldn't share any

of that information with a stranger he met ten minutes ago but the day had been so long and uncomfortable—everything about it was just so damned uncomfortable—that Nash figured what the hell? What's one more uncomfortable moment in a sea of them? Or maybe he was just too exhausted to care about things like boundaries.

"I have a brother, Mason, who's only a few years younger than me. He and my mom are back in Clarksville, and my dad died when I was twelve. Oh, and no pets."

Jake had stopped making up his bunk and stood to look at Nash. Nash prepared himself for the usual question that came when people found out his dad was dead: how did he die?

Instead, Jake replied, "No pets! What the hell? That's un-American, man. I'm keeping my eye on you, Kaplan," and, grinning, went back to making up the bottom bunk.

Outside their room, they could hear the clatter and yelling from around the dorms. But Nash was becoming numb to the sounds of raised voices. He took advantage of the opportunity to look around his room and noticed the bleakness of the cement was broken up by a large picture window that took up the majority of one of the walls. It was covered up by boring, beige hotel-like curtains. Although it was too dark to make out the mountains, Nash knew they were there. A third wall contained two built-in wardrobes, one for him, the other for Jake. Each wardrobe had a place to hang clothes, and floor-to-ceiling shelves to put more stuff. There were built-in drawers under the bottom bunk bed, two for each of them. On the final wall, Nash saw a pair of built-in desks, with rollaway desk chairs, and wall-mounted bookshelves over each. This would be home for the next six weeks, maybe the next four years.

The stark contrast between this room and Nash's room back home couldn't be ignored. He had traded in all the comforts of his life, his old truck, his friends, his free time, his computer, his cell phone, his ability to stand whatever way he wanted and look at whatever the hell he wanted for this . . . *experience*. For what? For his dead father? For his mom and brother? For a town of people who had known him and his family for decades? Yes. He didn't want to let any of them down. Yes, he wanted to be an officer and a pilot like his dad was during the wars in Afghanistan and Iraq. But he also wanted to see what he was made of, and the Academy seemed like as good a place as any to test himself.

An upperclassman's voice cut through Nash's thoughts and rang through the hallways, "LIGHTS OUT, PRINCESSES. GET TO YOUR RACKS."

Nash jumped up into his bunk, lay on the unmade mattress, and covered himself with the scratchy government-green blanket. He was still in his clothes and hadn't brushed his teeth. The coolness of the naked plastic pillow felt weird against his shaved head. It would be two more days before he would get the chance to brush his teeth or make up his bunk.

CHAPTER 4

"**P**ing!" Nash said, after he ran up to the waiting upperclassman, and came to attention.

"Okay, Kaplan. Go back and report. Pong."

Nash did an about-face and ran back across the length of the parade field where he'd left the other upperclassmen. *You would think after three weeks of basic training, the bastards would find something more creative than treating us like human ping-pong balls*, Nash thought as he ran. He was starting to think of them with a dull hatred, like the hatred he had for his combat boots. They were sonsabitches that he had to deal with every day.

But he was getting used to it. It was amazing what Nash had grown used to in just three short weeks.

When he finally arrived in front of the other upperclassman, Nash reported, "Pong."

Nash was just about done. Ready to ring out, tap out, sign out, whatever-out he needed to do to get back on the bus that headed to Clarksville. Why did he think this was a good idea, anyway? He could have gone to the local community college in Clarksville. He could have gotten a good job in town, while still enjoying his freshman year of college like everyone else back home—those that were going to college. Just because his mom couldn't afford to help him with college was no reason to put up with this place, right? Lots of kids took out student loans . . . and then worked the next twenty years of their lives trying to pay them off (if they were lucky enough to land a job out of college). He didn't *have* to be an officer in the Air Force. Just because he had ideas of following in his dad's footsteps didn't mean he was supposed to put up with this shit. Besides, his dad never talked about his time at the Academy when Nash was a kid. Nash wouldn't have even known he went there if he hadn't found his "Class of '95" ring in a keepsake box in his mom's closet. When he asked his mom about it, she couldn't really tell him much. They had met right after he graduated. He was visiting his brother Frank in Clarksville for the summer, and they fell for each other—or something like that. Nash couldn't imagine his dad putting up with this shit anyway. He had flown the F-15E Strike Eagle into places no one else would go. His dad was badass. But Nash didn't feel very badass acting like a ping-pong ball while all these assholes snickered at him. He felt like quitting. But he hadn't yet.

"Looks like we found something Kaplan can do," the upperclassman said to no one in particular. Some of the other upperclassmen chuckled, but their good time was short-lived as soon as Smokey arrived on the scene. He called the mean-spirited cadet over with a quick lift of his chin, and even though Nash couldn't hear what Smokey said to him, the cadet came back much less high-spirited than before.

"Go away, smack," the cadet mumbled. And with that, Nash was dismissed and ran off to join the rest of his flight in the middle of the parade field. Nash had learned that Smokey had no time for shenanigans from anyone, no matter if you were only a freshman Doolie like Nash or an upperclassman.

When Nash caught up with his flight, he quickly spotted the familiar faces of Greene and Suleyman, or Sully. Greene was from Los Angeles, and some of the other basics had started calling her "Hollywood" because they were unimaginative assholes. Suleyman was a high-society kid from Connecticut, by way of the Sudan. The Suleymans were refugees who had come to America during one of their nation's civil wars. Sully had been in the United States since he was twelve, and he had a positive outlook about absolutely *everything*. He might have been the only person who enjoyed every aspect of the Academy, even including basic training and zero-five hundred wakeups. Nash guessed waking up without gunfire all around gave Sully cause to smile.

Despite the hectic schedule, Nash and Jake had made fast friends with Greene and Sully during details, the duties assigned to each basic cadet to keep the dorms from becoming cesspools of filth. The foursome was currently assigned to trash detail, responsible for taking out bags and bags of trash to the dumpsters every morning. Nash learned a lot about Sully and Greene in those two and three minute strolls back and forth.

Per usual, Sully greeted Nash with a toothy smile as Nash ran up to the group, and despite the earlier bullshit annoyance of upperclassmen using him as a ping-pong ball, Nash couldn't help but smile back. He was beginning to count on Sully's smile, Jake's ridiculous wit, and Greene's willingness to work until the job was done. Almost without realizing it, Nash had formed a little basic-training family in the last twenty-one days.

"KAPLAN! WHAT ARE YOU DOING?" the drill instructor yelled. "GET IN FORMATION!" Without hesitation, Nash jumped into position, and prepared to march the six miles into what the cadets called "Jack's Valley."

This trip would mark the final two weeks of training before Nash and the other basics would march in the Acceptance Parade. Soon, they would no longer be basic cadets. With each week that passed, Nash was getting further and further into basic training, and closer and closer to being finished with it. With each step into the Valley, Nash moved further away from who he was on the first day at the Academy: an unprepared kid too focused on the negatives of training. Nash felt like each step brought him closer to who he wanted to be when he graduated from the

Academy: a Second Lieutenant in the United States Air Force.

"FORWARD, MARCH!" The drill instructor called the command for the flight to move forward, and without thinking, Nash fell into step with the cadence.

"HUT, TWO, THREE, FOUR! HUT, TWO, THREE, FOUR!" The clipped phrases of the other drill instructors rang across the mass of a few hundred basic cadets as they all moved in unison toward the pine tree-lined trails entering Jack's Valley. Without warning, Nash was overcome by a surge of emotion as he felt the rumble of a hundred footsteps beneath his feet. From studying the blue book, he knew that every class who had ever attended the Academy since 1954 had made this same march. Every man and woman who had made it this far in training had placed their footsteps along the same paths that Nash's feet were treading. He felt the history of what he was doing at that moment, and he pulled his shoulders back a little straighter and held his head a little higher. Right then, Nash wasn't thinking about quitting, he wasn't thinking about the zero-five hundred wakeups, or the asshole upperclassmen who treated him like shit. He wasn't thinking about his sad little room where everything had to be neatly folded or placed in the exact right spot. He wasn't thinking about Smokey scaring the shit out of him, or how much he missed home. He was thinking about joining a legacy.

CHAPTER

5

*D*ear Mom,

We have one more week in Jack's Valley before we march in the Acceptance Parade. We've already spent a week here, camping, hiking, practicing drill, and I'm having a lot of fun. There are lots of trees and we're sleeping in tents that are big enough to hold like 60 cots. Remember that time Mason and I went camping with Uncle Frank in Cottonwood Hills? It's just like that. Campfires every night, lots of food. I'm eating plenty and sleeping great.

Thank you so much for sending the cookies.

Everyone loved them. I will call as soon as I
can. I love you.
Nash

Nash imagined his mom reading his letter aloud to Mason, and his brother knowing it was mostly bullshit because they had hated that trip with their uncle, which is why they never went again. Nash had been stung by red ants when they went hiking and Mason nearly fell headfirst into a snake's nest. But Nash wasn't concerned about Mason's feelings; he was concerned about their mom's. He didn't want her worrying about him getting enough to eat or enough rest. She might write an email to the Commandant of Cadets, and Nash assumed the General had more important things to do than answer emails from his mom.

Nash planned to write Mason his own letter. He really missed his brother. Growing up, it was always just the two of them. As far back as Nash could remember, Mason had been by his side. Nash was always showing him how to do stuff like tie his shoes, ride a bike, write in cursive, make a fart noise with his armpit, beat the next level of Super Mario World, start a fire with newspapers in the kitchen trash can, and then how to work the fire extinguisher. Nash was the father figure Mason had missed after their dad died. They had their Uncle Frank, but he moved to Tennessee when the boys were little, and didn't get back to Clarksville more than a few times a year.

Nash wanted to tell Mason everything about the Academy, but there just wasn't enough time before lights out to write down all the stuff that was in Nash's head. Besides, Nash hadn't written an actual letter since fourth grade when his teacher made them be pen pals with some kids in France. Putting pen to real-life paper took a lot longer than shooting off an email or text message. Nash couldn't wait to get his phone back in a week, and then he could text Mason all the time.

But for now, he would have to settle for writing him letters.

Nash sat on his cot and began to write down everything he had wanted to tell his brother since he landed in Colorado. He wrote about the beauty of the mountains covered with fir trees. He wrote to him about the herd of elk he saw the day before as they were doing a five-mile ruck march along the trails. Then he wrote about the day-to-day shit.

This place sucks a lot, bro. We have to get up at five in the morning.

Nash continued writing about the lack of time they had to do stuff like brush their teeth, take a shower, and eat a damn sandwich. He complained about how they had to run everywhere, but then there was nothing to do when they got there but wait and wait with those fucking blue books in their faces. He told Mason what jerks the upperclassmen were and how he heard the sound of Smokey's footsteps in his dreams. Then he wrote about what the assholes did to the cookies his mom sent.

They sat down in front of the whole squad and ate them—every single one of them. I didn't get a single raisin from a single cookie. Then, they made us do push-ups because I got a care package with food in it.

Nash asked Mason to stop their mom from sending any more care packages. His arms couldn't handle the training. And as Nash wrote, a sort of realization came to him about how all this stuff was becoming . . . normal. He hadn't really had a chance to think about the stuff outside of his own head, and putting it on paper for his brother gave Nash the time to recognize that he was used to it. He guessed he was a little crazy now, too. When did this become regular?

He wrote about his new friends and how much he liked learning to march and working with all these basics to get stuff done.

Last week, we did this ropes course thing where we had to figure out how to get through this like spider web of ropes strung up between all these trees. The only way to get through it was to work together, lifting each other, relying on each other to catch you. This place is all about the teamwork. You're not even allowed to go to the john by yourself. You have to take a "battle buddy" in case you get lost in the woods or something.

Finally, he wrote about how he had wanted to quit—every day—in the beginning. He wrote about how the first three weeks he missed home so much he almost cried. He wrote about the forty or so other basics who had already quit because they couldn't take the yelling, or they missed their parents, or they wanted to get laid and drunk more than they wanted to finish basic training. He told his brother how he was jealous of them, but not enough to call it quits himself. He imagined them sleeping—like really sleeping—in a comfy bed without plastic sheets, or stuffing their faces with pizza, or downing some beers, and being allowed to enjoy life.

As Nash wrote about them, he thought, *they'll never know if it gets better.* They'll never be able to look back and think: *I did that.* Nash thought about the last person who quit the day before. They had just finished a terrible obstacle course where they'd climbed over splintered logs and crawled through freezing mud while carrying ten-pound, cement-filled rifles above their heads. It was a particularly brutal day of soggy boots, freezing fingers, and short tempers. One basic had evidently reached his breaking point. Nash had watched him pack up his stuff earlier that afternoon. Nash wanted to ask him what it felt like to quit. He wanted to know what had happened in his mind during that moment when he decided enough was enough. But he didn't ask.

Nash finished his letter, telling his brother how much he missed him and asking how everyone back home was doing.

Write back, okay? I love you, dork.

CHAPTER 6

"We will not lie, steal, cheat, nor tolerate anyone among us who does." The group of twenty-two basic cadets repeated the honor code to the Captain standing at the front of the room.

"Okay, you all seem to know what the code is, but what does it mean?" Captain Waters asked to no one in particular. It was the last day of Jack's Valley, and all the basics were more exhausted than when they began two weeks ago. All anyone wanted to do was make the six-mile trek back to The Hill, crawl into their bunks, and sleep for three days. Captain Waters's question was met with the sound of an errant cough and shuffling in the metal chairs.

Finally, after what felt like five minutes of Waters just staring at everyone, one of the basics raised his hand.

"Go ahead. What do those words mean?" Captain Waters nodded at him to give the answer.

"I dunno. I guess you don't want us to steal stuff from each other, or lie about stuff, or cheat or whatever," finished the articulate kid with an oily forehead.

Another basic chimed in, "And you want us to rat on each other." The basic cadet concluded to a few snickers and more shuffling in metal seats.

"You're almost right, Basic Cadet Newcomb." Captain Waters read the embroidered name on his military uniform. "Except I'm not sure you get the complexity and seriousness of the oath." She continued, "It's not that we expect you to *rat* out your fellow cadets. We expect you to be *honorable*. And the code gives you guidelines for what we mean by that. If you ever find yourself needing to make a difficult decision, we want the code to guide you."

Basic Cadet Newcomb confidently raised his hand again.

"Go ahead," Captain Waters said.

"Where I'm from, we don't snitch on each other. Snitches get stitches."

The class laughed, and Nash chuckled right along with them.

The basic kept on talking, "And for the past five weeks, y'all have been telling us to take care of each other. If one of us gets in trouble, we're all facedown doing push-ups."

The class groaned, and a chorus of "yeahs" started somewhere behind Nash's left shoulder. But Nash kept his eyes on Captain Waters. He noticed she was nodding along and almost smiling. She looked like she was actually enjoying the cadet's comments.

The basic continued, "Now you're teaching us

to tell on each other?" The class waited anxiously for Captain Waters's reaction.

"You're absolutely right, Basic Cadet Newcomb," Captain Waters answered. "We have spent many weeks trying to bring you together, to make you rely on each other. In fact, you've probably noticed we spend the majority of our training trying to instill a particular set of values and beliefs—Air Force values and beliefs—into each and every person who wants to become an airman. But not everyone makes the cut. Not everyone is able to change their attitudes about how they have done things in the past, and get on board with how we do things here in the Air Force. And that's okay, because the Air Force isn't for everyone."

Nash knew the code he and his friends had back home. It wasn't literally that snitches got stitches, but snitches definitely were shunned from the group. No one liked to have someone around they couldn't trust to keep their mouth shut in times of trouble. But at the Academy, they were being taught something else. He didn't really understand how they expected people to tell on each other. Nash continued to listen intently, almost leaning forward in his seat, waiting for the next words to come from her mouth. She was making it seem like she understood how hard this was to commit to—she made it seem like she understood they were human beings with minds of their own.

Captain Waters continued, "We believe that caring for one another means protecting one another from bad decisions. We want you to be guardrails for each other, and not let each other go off a cliff. It's not ratting each other out. It's about helping each other make good decisions that are in line with the code. It's something to really think about and decide whether or not you can do it. You'll take the honor oath during the Acceptance Parade."

With that, Captain Waters dismissed the

honor session and the basic cadets filed out of the room. Nash thought about what she said all the way to the chow tent.

As he entered the tent, his stomach emitted a bear-like growl and flip-flopped so hard that he almost felt sick. He was always starving here. Mealtimes felt like they were spaced thirty-six hours apart, and they lasted for three minutes. But Nash was getting pretty good at maximizing them.

That first week of basic had been beyond awful. Everything was a messy blur of sweat, stiff muscles, and extreme exhaustion. He couldn't even remember eating at all, but he knew he must have eaten something. After all, he was still alive. But all the rules to eating really frustrated the hell out of him and were enough to make him want to fly into a rage and throw his potato casserole and green bean delight across the chow hall. But, over time, he learned how to do it right through negative reinforcement.

"GET YOUR BACK OFF MY CHAIR, BASIC! WHAT DO YOU THINK THIS IS? A RESTAURANT? STOP RELAXING, EAT, AND GET OUT!" Nash remembered the thunder of Smokey's orders during those first mealtimes. He learned to sit up straight with his back miles away from the back of the seat.

"PUT YOUR FORK DOWN WHEN YOU'RE CHEWING, BASIC! ARE YOU AFRAID SOMEONE'S GOING TO STEAL YOUR MASHED POTATOES? DO YOU THINK EVERYONE HERE IS A THIEF? SET THAT FORK DOWN UNTIL YOUR MOUTH IS EMPTY!" That's how Nash learned to rest his fork at the edge of the plate until he was ready to take another bite.

"ARE YOU SPECIAL, BASIC? CLEARLY YOU THINK YOU'RE MORE SPECIAL THAN EVERYONE ELSE BECAUSE YOU GET TO HANG ONTO YOUR FORK WHILE EVERYONE ELSE HAS TO SET THEIR

FORKS DOWN BETWEEN BITES!" *Fling!* Smokey sent Nash's fork sailing across the chow hall where it came to a skittering halt against another basic's boots.

"KEEP YOUR FORK GROUNDED UNTIL YOU'VE TAKEN FIVE CHEWS, BASIC! SWALLOW AND LOAD. EAT LIKE A GODDAMN GENTLEMAN!" Smokey kindly instructed.

Nash had learned how to eat efficiently and quickly. He was able to finish his meal now sometimes before Smokey even made it to his table for training. Little successes like those kept Nash from quitting in the early days. Now, in the final moments of basic, Nash only thought about quitting once or twice a week. He guessed that was better than the twenty times a day he used to want to quit.

Nash was now a pro at completely blocking out the yelling. He had mastered mind-wandering where he'd go into a secluded space inside his mind and picture funny shit to keep him from curling up in a ball at Smokey's feet or punching one of the upperclassmen jerks in the face. He couldn't take all the credit for this newly acquired skill though. He'd actually learned it from Jake.

"Just picture their o-face," Jake told Nash during one of their brief bedtime conversations. The bedtime conversations were some of the best parts of basic training. They made Nash feel normal for a few minutes every day. Beginning each day with Greene and Sully, and ending with one of Jake's jokes and stories each night kept Nash sane. With those lights-out conversations, Nash learned more and more about Jake. He learned that Jake's dad was a retired Air Force general and his mom was some bigwig president of a telephone company in Houston. Jake was confident, funny, and unafraid of failure—mostly because it never occurred to him that he could fail.

"What's an o-face?" Nash asked a little confused.

"You know, the face you make when you're doing it, man. The o-o-o-face." Jake contorted his face.

"Gross, man! I don't want to see you do that ever again, and I don't even want to think of Smokey's o-face, or whatever you call it. He scares the shit out of me."

"What better way to obliterate your fear than to picture his o-face in your head, man? Trust me. Do it."

The next time Smokey came around Nash remembered Jake's advice, and he began to think of Smokey's o-face. He noticed the scrunched up eyes when he yelled, and the way he snarled like a pit bull when he was enraged. Instantly, he thought of Smokey snarling while having sex and Nash almost couldn't hold in his laughter.

Nash liked Jake. He liked Greene and Sully, too. Actually, Nash felt close to every basic cadet in his flight. They helped keep each other grounded through the seemingly nonsense training environment. They were all in it together, and when one of them was struggling, the others would help out if they could. Already Greene had organized study sessions in the day room—the common area where the cadets could come together since males weren't allowed in female rooms, and vice versa. Those who were having trouble memorizing the stuff in the blue book would meet up on the weekends, when the basics actually had some time to themselves, and practiced reciting quotes from dead military leaders.

Sully was great at drill and facing movements, so Nash could usually find him marching up and down the long corridors, helping some poor, uncoordinated kid learn how to do a proper about-face or Change Step in preparation for a drill competition. Jake could be counted on to offer a laugh, and he could fold a hospital corner on a bed sheet that would make General Patton jealous.

Nash was learning to depend on his friends more and more, and they already depended on him, too. Nash was known as the brains of the bunch, and several Doolies already warned him they would need his help with Calculus and Chemistry when classes started. He was really looking forward to classes, or academics, as they were known at the Academy. He knew they would be difficult, but he hoped that they would be easier to navigate than basic training.

The thing about the Academy that was so hard to explain to people who hadn't been through it wasn't necessarily the physical constraints. Yes, not being able to take a long shower was annoying. Not being able to lie in your bed all day on the weekend sucked, and not being able to use your cell phone was torturous, but the real difficulty was in the mental game. There was always someone watching you, always someone waiting to catch you doing something wrong. Nash was sick of being watched all the time, and he wanted to get inside the classroom where he hoped the watching stopped and the learning began.

CHAPTER 7

"Hey, mom!" Nash loved hearing his mom's voice through the phone. It felt like he left years ago, but it had only been a little over a month.

"Hi, Nash! How are you, honey? Are you doing okay? Do you need anything?" Hearing his mom's concern almost broke him. *Do not cry, Nash,* he reminded himself sternly as his mom rapid-fired questions at him.

"Yeah, mom. I'm doing okay. How are things at home? How's work going?" Nash wondered if his mom heard anything different in his voice, something she'd not heard before. He thought he still sounded like himself, but he wondered if he'd changed at all. His mom and Mason knew him better than anyone else, and Nash knew they were both a little concerned that being away from home would make him into someone different. His mom had even mentioned it before he got on the plane, "Don't change too much, Nash. I don't want that beautiful heart to change." At the time, he thought his mom was being a little overdramatic, but Nash wasn't so sure he hadn't become a little more distant, a little more cynical.

Nash heard his mom's voice tremble slightly as she replied, "Things are fine at the store. You know we're always so busy in August." Nash's mom managed a Golf and Games center, and summer was filled with groups of camp kids taking field trips, harried parents hanging on until school started up again, and teens spending their summer job cash in the laser tag tournaments.

Nash missed his mom so much. He felt like a kid dropped off at the first day of kindergarten. *Get it together, Nash*, he thought to himself. He knew his mom wouldn't think her steady, solid son would be so affected by being so far away from his family. She didn't know how his removal from regular society made him appreciate all the quiet moments he had walking through the cornfields around their house. She didn't know he missed the four walls of his bedroom. She definitely didn't know he even missed cutting the grass. And she couldn't imagine how much he wanted to see her face.

"Mom, I've almost made it through. The Acceptance Parade is tomorrow," Nash's voice was excited, but tired, too.

"I know, honey! We've got a calendar on the fridge, and we're counting down the days until winter break." Nash could hear the excitement in her voice. He couldn't wait to head home in a few months and get a big hug. His mom gave the best hugs. She didn't hold anything back, and she never pulled away first.

"Oh yeah. I can't wait for that, too. Is Mason

around? I only have a couple minutes and I want to talk him."

"Sorry, hon. He's still at baseball practice. I'll tell him you called, though. Will you be able to call again?"

"I don't know. They don't really give us a schedule." Nash chuckled at his own bad joke. "Tell Mason I miss him, and I'll call you again as soon as I can. Hey, Mom, could you mail me my soccer cleats? They should be in my closet somewhere."

"Sure, I will. I'll mail them off tomorrow. So, tell me how things are going . . . have you made many friends? How are classes going?"

"We're not in class yet. We won't start until Monday." The upperclassmen were starting to shoo the basics off their cell phones. Nash thought he heard Smokey's footsteps coming down the hallway. He hurried to answer his mom's questions, "I've made some pretty good friends, so far, but I can't really go into details, Mom. My time is up. I'll tell you about them next time, okay? I love you and I miss you. Send the cleats soon, okay? Bye, Mom."

CHAPTER

8

The next day, Nash stood with a few hundred other basics and prepared to march in the Acceptance Parade. His feet felt like they were on fire inside the high-gloss black shoes he was wearing with his uniform. The Colorado sun, even though it was much gentler than the Indiana summer sun, still found its way through the glossy black plastic and baked whatever was inside—in this case, Nash's toes. He felt like he was standing in a puddle of hot lava, and it was crawling all over the sides and tops of his feet. He tried scrunching his toes to provide some relief. Nothing. He tried imagining the o-faces of those around him.

Nothing. He switched the weight from his right leg to his left leg, and then back again slowly. That helped a little bit. What would really help would be to start marching.

"Fuck, it's hot as shit out here," Jake whispered to Nash. He stood directly behind him in the formation. "When are they starting this dog and pony show, for fuck's sake? We've been out here for hours waiting for this shit to start. I can't even recognize a face in the crowd, not a single face. I could've paid some hippy kid to put on this uniform, tuck his man-bun inside this hat, and stand here in my place and no one would've known any better."

Hearing Jake complaining brought a smile to Nash's face. Jake usually said what Nash was really thinking but was too polite to say out loud.

"SQUADRON! ATTENTION!"

Finally, the parade was about to begin, and Nash's feet would find some relief.

"FORWARD MARCH! COLUMN RIGHT, MARCH!"

As the Cadet Wing Commander (some dude Nash had never met) called out the commands to get the Doolies moving, Nash thought about the honor oath he was about to take. He thought about the way Captain Waters had stressed the importance of taking the code seriously, and really thinking about whether each of them could commit to abiding by it. Nash had thought about it for the last several days. The night before, at lights out, he asked Jake how he felt about taking the honor code.

"Who the fuck cares about the code, dude? Just say the shit they want you to say, and get the fuck on with it," was Jake's attitude.

But Nash wasn't so sure he could do that. He was raised that his word was important, and if he didn't have his word, he didn't have much at all. Besides, he didn't really want to go through all this shit for the last five weeks if it meant nothing. He didn't want to go through this shit for the next year if it wasn't real. So, he had actually been thinking about it.

It wasn't the lying, stealing, and cheating that was giving him something to think about. It was the toleration part. Could he snitch on someone? Amongst Nash's friends back home, he knew that calling someone out was just as bad as doing it yourself. Nash couldn't really make the two parts of the code marry up to each other.

"Listen, dude," Jake had continued his counsel last night. "The way I think about it, every single person will have taken this oath just like you. Every single one of these sonsabitches is promising not to lie, or fuckin' cheat, or steal shit. So if one of them does, they've already broke their promise, right? So fuck 'em. They don't deserve any loyalty after that."

Somehow that bit of perspective made sense to Nash. That's where the two friends had left it as the lights went out, but Nash still wasn't sure how he felt about actually carrying through with it, if he ever had to make the choice.

But the time is now, folks, Nash thought as he marched firmly toward the adjutant stand where the cadets would make their statement in front of the Commandant.

After a "SQUADRON, HALT! RIGHT FACE!" from the Cadet Group Commander, Nash raised his right hand and swore an oath with the other basics, "I will not lie, steal, or cheat, nor tolerate among us anyone who does. Furthermore, I resolve to do my duty and to live honorably."

After the parade, the basic cadets were no longer "basics." They were bona fide Air Force Academy Cadets: Doolies. Nash was enjoying the momentary reprieve from all the yelling. The very people who had yelled in his face the day before were now standing around shaking hands with parents and other family as if they hadn't been assholes to their son or daughter twenty-four hours ago. It was so bizarre.

"Cadet Kaplan! It's so wonderful to meet you. Jake has told us how you keep him out of trouble." Jake's mom laughed at her own comment, as Nash joined Jake and his parents. Nash was a little intimidated to be standing so close to such a high-ranking person as Jake's dad. He had never met a general before.

Nash quickly replied, "Oh, I'm not sure what he's talking about, Mrs. Nichols. I haven't seen him get into any trouble."

"Humph," The general grunted in disbelief, casually raising an eyebrow.

It was strange to watch Jake around his parents. He became quieter. He became polite, and a little withdrawn. Nash planned to ask him about it later. *Maybe they had a fight or something*, he thought.

But the really interesting thing to watch was how everyone else responded to his parents, particularly Jake's dad. Many of the basic training cadre, the upperclassmen and the military training instructors who blistered Nash's eardrums on a daily basis were laughing and joking with Jake's dad. It seemed that so many people knew who he was without needing an introduction.

"I wish we could get the fuck out of here." Jake was suddenly right beside Nash. "I wish we could get lit tonight. You know?"

Nash did know, now that Jake brought it up. Funny. Nash hadn't even thought of beer for the last six weeks. He had thought about sleep. And more sleep. He had thought about his quiet room, and what his buddies were doing back home. He had thought about his little brother and his mom missing him. But he hadn't thought about beer. Until now. Damn Jake.

"Too bad we're not twenty-one, dude," Nash threw back at him.

"That's not a problem I can't handle, Kaplan." Jake raised his eyebrow like a bad guy on television.

"Yeah, right. We're going to go through all the hell of the last six weeks, and then at the first opportunity to mess it up, we do it. No thanks,

Nichols." Nash returned the favor and called Jake by his last name as he felt a bead of sweat take off down his spine.

Jake took a step back and smiled a crooked grin. "Gotcha," he said.

Nash chuckled and turned back toward General and Mrs. Nichols. Nash was shocked to see who had joined their group. They were talking to Smokey. Nash's Spidey senses hadn't alerted him that he was so close. Damnit.

"How do your parents know Smokey?" Nash quietly asked Jake, but he was no longer standing beside him. He watched Jake walk away toward Sully and his family standing several feet away.

For some reason Nash still wasn't sure he could clearly explain, he decided it was time to push the limits. There had been times in Nash's life where a feeling of recklessness came upon him. Once he streaked across the ice rink during a hockey game as part of a dare from his buddies. That didn't end well. When he was a sophomore he decided to ask a senior to prom, which wouldn't have been so bad except she had a very large, very athletic senior boyfriend. That didn't end well, either. Why Nash thought this moment would be better than his past experiences, he had no idea. But before he could stop himself, he took a few steps forward and found himself within the conversation circle that included Smokey the Bear.

Mrs. Nichols smiled brightly at him and said, "Cadet Kaplan! I'm sure you've met our friend, Manni, er Sergeant Mancini—probably to you. Manni, did you terrify Cadet Kaplan or are you getting gentler in your old age?" she teased. She was teasing Smokey. And he smiled back at her. He fucking smiled. *What the hell*, Nash internally shrugged, *I'm going for it.*

"Sergeant Mancini was a big ole teddy bear, ma'am," Nash never took his eyes from his reflection in Smokey's aviator sunglasses. He thought he saw Smokey's jaw muscles clench down tightly, and, just as quickly, they released like a snake who swallowed its prey. Nash swallowed hard.

Before Smokey could respond, General Nichols belly-laughed and clamped his giant hand on Nash's shoulder. It felt like it weighed twenty pounds. "Bet you've never been called that before, Manni. Certainly not by one of your trainees." General Nichols laughed some more.

"Nope. Can't say that I have—maybe I am getting soft." His stare never left Nash's face. "I'll have to tighten up from now on."

What? Did Nash hear him right? From now on? He thought they were through the training part of basic. Were there new recruits coming in? Is that what Smokey meant? Nash felt another bead of sweat race down his back, and he wanted to lie down.

"Wh-what happens from now on?" Nash asked.

Mrs. Nichols turned to Sergeant Mancini, "Manni! You're not telling them what comes after basic training? When did that change?"

"We tell them," Smokey said, his smile growing wider. "It's Doolie year."

"Yes, but it doesn't seem like young Kaplan knows what to expect," General Nichols chimed in.

"No, it doesn't." Smokey grinned.

"Cadet Kaplan, I'll tell you if this big teddy bear won't." Mrs. Nichols took one of Nash's hands into hers, as if she was about to give him a tragic diagnosis. "Now that basic training is over, you're officially a Four Degree, a Doolie."

Nash felt rivulets of sweat making their way down the backs of his legs. Was he pissing on himself? Surely not. He hadn't done that since the time he was playing outfield when he was five and coach wouldn't let him go the restroom until the inning was over. Big mistake.

"So, what's the big deal about that? Isn't that what we're here for? I mean, to be Doolies?" Nash asked nervously, his lips sticking to his teeth as he tried to smile.

"Yes, of course," Mrs. Nichols continued. "But you won't be protected by the cadre anymore."

Nash laughed out loud—the first good laugh he'd had in six weeks. "Yeah, right. Protected!" He guffawed, and then his laugh dwindled and died as he looked from Mrs. Nichols's face to General Nichols's face, finally resting on Smokey's wide grin. "What do you mean by *protected?*"

"While you were in basic, only the cadre could train you. Now that you're finished with basic, all the upperclassmen will ensure you're learning everything you need to know. They will all be part of your training now."

Holy shitballs was all that kept ringing through Kaplan's head. There were at least two hundred fifty upperclassmen in his squadron alone. And there were almost ten squadrons in the entire cadet wing. That meant there were about three thousand upperclassmen Nash had been protected from during basic training. Starting tomorrow, Nash would no longer belong only to the cadre.

He and his friends would be fair game for any junior or senior who had the time and inclination to teach them something. Shitballs didn't seem a harsh enough expletive to have echoing through his mind. How was he going to get through the semester if he had to worry about school and the thousands of asshole upperclassmen waiting in the wings to put him in the "forward leaning rest position," otherwise known as a push-up? If Nash hadn't been grateful for his Academy friends before, he was fully in love with them now. Together, they would have to figure out how to make it through this first semester.

CHAPTER 9

"I'm feeling quizzy today. It's an emotion I've been feeling a lot lately," Dr. Maynard, the chemistry professor stated.

Nash's chemistry class shuffled loudly in their seats. One or two students groaned.

"Clear your desks!" While Dr. Maynard passed out the quiz, Nash shot a quick look over at Jake. Nash knew Jake was worried about what another F in Chem would mean to his GPA. He also knew Jake and he were up all night writing a fifteen-pager on Charlemagne and Western Europe (which was probably going to be a disappointing grade for Nash because he didn't know what he actually wrote down), and neither of them had opened a chemistry book all night.

The back of the quiz, the clean white piece of paper, intimidated Nash like walking up to a cliff before a bungee jump. As soon as the class turned it over, some of them would be fucked. Nash dismally watched Maynard as he made his way around the room, from cadet to cadet, passing out the quiz.

"Okay, begin," Maynard said. Nash's hand actually trembled a little as he reached for the corner of the page and flipped it over.

Thank God was his initial thought. There were only two questions. But that relief didn't last long when Nash read the first one:

1. An experiment is performed to study the following unimolecular reaction:

$A \leftrightarrow B$

Starting with 3.00 moles of A in a confined vessel of volume 3.00 L, the initial rate of formation of B is found to be 0.020 M/s. When the system finally reaches equilibrium, 1.00 mole of B is obtained. What is the rate constant of the reverse process (B $\leftrightarrow$ A)?

What the fuck? Nash thought. He should get a t-shirt that said WTF and wear it underneath his dress blues every single day. It was basically the only phrase he used nearly every minute of every day. It was the only phrase that made sense to him in this school sometimes. It was also the only phrase that rang through his brain each time the alarm clock went off at zero five hundred hours, each time an upperclassman got in his face, each time he sat down in one of these science-minded classes, each time another Graded Review— what they called tests at the Academy—was announced, and each time he had to take a quiz.

Nash looked up from the quiz and caught Jake's furtive glance and watched him mouth the word "Fuck" across the room. Nash knew

Jake wasn't strong in Chemistry. Nash, Greene, and Sully had started meeting two or three times a week as a study group, and it seemed to help them understand the material and keep track of what was due in what class. Jake came sometimes, but not as often as the other three.

Nash looked around the classroom as everyone else wrote frantically, bit the heads off their erasers, or chewed their fingernails to the nubs. No one in this school had fingernails anymore. If basic training didn't give them enough to stress about, classes did. Everyone here walked around with bloody cuticles and crazy eyes. Nash felt sweat form on his upper lip. Dr. Maynard made eye contact with him, and Nash quickly dropped his eyes back to the page. Skipping the first question, Nash hoped he could score some easier points with question two.

2. Write the equilibrium expression for the following:

(a) solid calcium hydroxide dissolving in water

(b) dinitrogen pentoxide decomposing into nitrogen dioxide and oxygen

(c) methane plus water forming carbon monoxide and hydrogen

(d) Haber process

Shit. Nash really needed that t-shirt. Dr. Maynard kept his eyes roaming around the room, lingering a little longer on Nash.

"Hey, dude. How's it going?" Nash greeted Jake as he walked in from boxing class. "Did you kick any upperclassman ass today?" Nash smiled at his own joke.

"Naw, not today. Got my ass handed to me by Williams again." Jake often boxed upperclassmen in his weight class. He was one of the boxing recruits on the Academy's team. In the few bouts that Nash was able to attend, he hadn't seen Jake land more than a single punch on anyone before he was consistently pummeled to the mat.

Nash had learned that Jake started boxing in the hoity-toity boarding school his parents sent him to—it was expected that he learned the sport in preparation for his attendance at the Academy. Over the weeks of getting to know Jake, Nash also learned that he was often expected to do what his parents wanted him to do.

"I'm going to take a piss. I'll be back and we'll head to chow, sound good?" Jake didn't wait for Nash to reply. He was already headed to the latrine.

Nash took the minute of quiet to sink into his desk chair. He wished he could lie down on his bed and take a nap, but he wasn't allowed to yet. If an upperclassman came by and caught him, he'd be up shit creek. Instead, he laid his head on the back of the chair and swiveled back and forth slightly. He took a few deep breaths in and raised his head and opened his eyes. Right before him was his calendar. He smiled a little at the picture at the top of the month of November: a pumpkin-colored Lotus Elise Series Two Roadster hugging the turns of some winding mountain road.

Like someone would ever take that beauty on a winding road up a mountain, Nash thought. But it was still a badass roadster. As Nash was day-dreaming about speeding around a racetrack in the Lotus, something he'd written on the calendar caught his eye: *CHEM GR!!!!!!!!* It was written in thick, black marker covering the entire square for November fourteenth—the next day. *What the fuck?*

"You ready?" Jake was standing at the door of their room.

No, I'm not ready, Nash thought. He wasn't ready for the Chem GR. He hadn't been studying because he thought he had another week. He'd been working on the history paper and trying to stay caught up in Calc and all the other classes he was taking. But Nash knew that Jake wasn't talking about tomorrow's GR.

"Yeah, let's go. I'm starving," he replied as he pushed his body up out of the chair and followed Jake to the chow hall. "Have you been studying for the Chem GR tomorrow?"

"Fuck you, Kaplan. That's not even funny, dude. The GR isn't until next week."

"No. I just saw it on the calendar. I have it marked as tomorrow." Nash delivered the blow as gently as he could, but Jake exploded anyway.

"You've gotta be fucking kidding me! I'm fucked. I can't get ready for the GR by tomorrow! I flunked the quiz last week." Nash could easily read the panic all over Jake's face.

Nash hoped to talk Jake down from the cliff. "Okay, dude. We've pulled all-nighters before, we can do it again." Was he trying to keep Jake calm, or himself?

Jake's panicked voice continued. "Maybe

Greene will be able to give us some scoop on the GR. She would have taken it today, right? Since we're on opposite schedules?" Jake referred to the alternating academic schedules where some students took classes on one day and the other half of students took the same classes on the next day, known as an "M day/T day" schedule.

But everyone knew they weren't allowed to discuss any GR information until the academic release date, which was usually the day after every freshman had taken the GR. Jake asking Greene for any information was treading dangerous waters.

Nash shrugged his shoulders and looked sideways at Jake. "C'mon, dude. You know she can't tell us anything that was on the GR. We'll just stock up on caffeine and Doritos and study the chapters that Maynard gave us on the study guide."

Jake jabbed at Nash with his elbow. "I wasn't going to ask for specifics, asshole," he tried to play it off. "I just wanted to know if the study guide was worth it, you know? Like that Maynard wasn't giving us bullshit."

Nash relaxed his shoulders, not realizing that they had tensed up. "Okay. We can ask Greene if the study guide's worth it. We'll quiz each other after chow."

"Sounds good," Jake replied as they stepped inside the doors of the chow hall.

———————

Nash and Jake stayed up well past lights out quizzing each other and cramming for the Chem GR. As they flipped pages back and forth, trying to memorize formulas, reactions, and chemical families, Jake seemed to be in a full-on panic. When Nash quizzed him on the stuff from the study guide, Jake only knew a few formulas.

Jake's downward spiral continued as the night wore on. "I'm fucked," Jake said. "If I fail this

GR, I'll be on academic probation. If I'm on academic probation, I won't be able to box, and if I can't box, I'll miss the tournament next month—my dad's coming to watch. Fuck. What am I going to do?"

———————

In the wee hours of the morning, as the sky was turning pink with the sun's rise, Nash was dreaming that he was running from a zombie—not like the zombies from that television show that Mason loved to watch, but the type from those Japanese horror flicks where they walked on all fours, upside down. In his dream, Nash was running through a mansion with never-ending hallways, trying to escape these weird animal zombies, but he was running through molasses or something. His legs wouldn't go fast enough and the zombies were always right behind him. He was also trying to remind himself to cup his hands and keep his heels together when he would stop to catch his breath. Just when Nash could smell the rancid decay of the zombie's rotting flesh getting stronger and stronger, closer and closer, his eyes jerked open.

He was on the top bunk of his dorm room.

He was not in a mansion.

There was no zombie chasing him.

There was a light on in the room. Nash turned his head slightly and saw Jake sitting at his desk, with his back to him. Nash released the breath he had been holding and tried to quiet the pounding of his heartbeat. *Damn*, he thought. He hadn't had a nightmare like that since he was a kid. This place was really messing with his brain, making him dream of zombies and shit. If he was more analytical, he might try to decipher the symbolism. He might try to equate the mansion with the Academy, and the zombies with the upperclassmen that made their lives nightmarish. Nash wouldn't say the Academy was a full-on nightmare, because they weren't all awful human beings, just most of them.

Maybe the zombies were the GRs they had to take all the time, each one looming larger than the last one. Maybe the zombies represented each day they were here. Nash knew the Academy was a stark contrast to other freshman-year college experiences elsewhere with keg parties and lots of girls—yeah, some tough classes, but nothing like the shit he and Jake dealt with last night.

As if Jake could read Nash's mind, he flung himself back in his chair and let out a sigh. He grabbed his head in both his hands and vigorously rubbed his face.

"You okay, dude?"

Jake jerked violently when he heard Nash's voice.

"Fuck! You scared the shit out of me, clown!"

"Sorry, man. I just had this messed-up dream about a dog zombie chasing me or something, and it woke me up."

"Sure, dude. You know you've been watching me from your ivory tower for hours now, pervert. And now you've ruined my chair because you seriously made me shit myself with your creepiness." Jake's humor never faltered, but he sounded run-down.

Nash laughed. "You better get some sleep, man. You've got about ninety minutes before the alarm goes off." Nash gestured to the alarm clock next to Jake's bunk.

"Seriously? I didn't realize it was so late already. I think I'm just going to pull an all-nighter at this point. If I try to sleep now, I'll just feel hungover all day, without the fun of getting there for real."

"Suit yourself," Nash said as he covered his head with the GI blanket.

"Is the light bothering you, Your Highness? I can study by flashlight if the prince is disturbed," Jake joked.

"Shut up, asshole," Nash joked back and rolled over to go back to sleep.

The blare of the alarm came too early for Nash, as it always did. He groaned and hit the snooze button but knew there was no time for snoozing. He had to be at breakfast in fifteen minutes, and he had to dress, shave, and complete his details before that. Mornings were the toughest times for Nash. He questioned his choice to attend a military school the most in the mornings when the alarm went off. It wasn't natural for people to wake up at zero-five hundred hours. Back home, Nash's friends weren't getting up at dawn unless they were heading to the creek for some fishing. They were sleeping soundly in their beds.

But each time the alarm went off, Nash also knew he was doing something that would bring him one step closer to becoming an Air Force officer. He knew he was doing something that brought him closer to his father.

Nash had thought about his dad more over the last few months at the Academy than he had in years. Right after his death, all Nash did was think about him. He wanted to remember everything his dad had ever told him—every story, every joke, every moment. But, of course, he couldn't. He would have written it all down if he had known he wouldn't see him again. But he didn't know that day would be the last time his dad would walk out to his truck, hug and kiss them all, and say, "I'll be back before you know it."

In the years since his dad's death, Nash had lost so many memories, despite his and Mason's best efforts to keep them fresh in their minds. They used to spend part of every day in a sort of "dad review," where they would start with "Remember when dad . . . " and fill in as many memories as they could. But over time, they found that they were repeating the same memories over and over. And eventually, new memories formed—memories of Mason hitting his first double, or Nash taking driving lessons with his mom, or the boys' first days of high school. It wasn't that Nash forgot about his dad; he was always there—a shadowy mist covering every happy moment. But over time, Nash stopped remembering him so much, and the sadness of his being gone changed to something else. Nash was still trying to figure it out. Maybe walking the campus where his dad went, experiencing the same traditions his dad experienced, would help Nash know him in a new way . . .

The alarm sounded again, startling Nash out of his reverie. "Shit!" Nash exclaimed as he noted he only had seven minutes to get ready for chow. The upperclassmen would be lined up at the doors, watching for anyone walking in late. Yesterday, Nash watched some poor bastard being quizzed over the blue book the moment he hit the doors, while he was in line getting his food, and even between bites of spaghetti and meatballs. What looked to be about fifty of them swarmed around the Doolie while everyone else was relieved it wasn't happening to them.

With that memory fresh, Nash ran to the bathroom to shave. He definitely wasn't trying to experience *that* tradition.

———

Now that they were out of basic training, Nash and the other Doolies were allowed to have their cell phones. This was both a great thing and an awful thing for Nash. It was great because he felt like he was almost back in the land of the living.

He could tweet again, and check out pics on Instagram. He could message his brother regularly through Facebook and texts like a normal person. And even though they couldn't take their cell phones into the academic buildings, he still felt like a human being when he was able to check his messages in his dorm room every night.

The negative side also came when he was able to check his messages in his dorm room every night. During basic, the whole world was shut out, and a new one was created that consisted of only what the Academy wanted them to learn and do. Nash didn't have to deal with all the fun his buddies back home were having; he didn't even have time to imagine it because the days were so packed with details, training, classes, and study groups. Now, with his cell phone, he couldn't get away from all the fun his buddies were having.

For example, Mason went camping last weekend with Nash's friend Jimmy and the group. Fuckers. Nash knew what kind of fun they had because it was the same fun they always had: drinking beers, telling stories, and doing dumb shit like jumping into the pond in their underwear or getting their trucks and jeeps stuck in the mud. Later, they would huddle around a campfire doing a whole lot of nothing, which sounded like heaven to Nash. The pictures Jimmy posted showed a lot of smiling friends, muddy jeeps, and no upperclassmen. *Yes, please*, thought Nash. He just wanted one weekend where he wasn't studying his ass off, or doing some military drill training—just one weekend where he could sleep past zero-seven hundred hours, and get in his truck and drive for hours and hours through the Colorado Mountains. It seemed such a waste to set this school down in the middle of the Front Range and then never let the students enjoy it.

He didn't want to post pics of him marching around in a circle, or completion of the perfect hospital corner he'd finally mastered on his top bunk. What was he going to tweet? How they slept on top of their covers every night so they wouldn't have to make their beds in the morning? How he studied until midnight every single day because classes were kicking his ass? Maybe how much fun it was to eat in the chow hall where Doolies had to recite the news stories of the day for the upperclassmen before morning meal? Somehow, Nash didn't think it would bring the same kind of happy feelings if his buddies back home knew what freshman year was like for him.

But seeing the pictures of Jimmy and the gang hanging out, just like Jimmy and Nash used to do senior year and every year before that in high school, also made Nash aware of how nothing had really changed for Jimmy back home. Yes, Jimmy was married and going to community college, and that was all well and good, but Nash knew that he wasn't stepping outside of his comfort zone. He was still surrounded by people who thought like him, read the same books, came from the same background, and experienced the same things. Nash was willing to bet that Jimmy had never sat in an auditorium with six hundred other people while a Medal of Honor recipient told his stories of surviving in a POW camp for six years during the Vietnam War. And Jimmy didn't know he was missing out on meeting amazing people like Sully, who knew four languages by the time he was twelve, or Jake who had traveled to seven different countries before he graduated high school. It's not that Nash thought his hometown and the people in it weren't good enough for him anymore. For the first twelve years of his life, he had moved around from base to base, always the "new kid," and he felt instantly at home in Clarksville when they moved back there after his dad died. He loved Clarksville and the people in it. He was just so amazed that they didn't want to know the whole rest of the world that was out there to explore. Jimmy and the rest of his friends seemed so happy to stay close to what they knew while all Nash could think of was how to expand and explore everything that he didn't know. He had been different from his friends in that way for a long time.

Nash had already experienced more than most of his friends as soon as he stepped foot on the airplane in Indianapolis. None of his friends had ever been to Colorado, or anywhere outside of the tri-state area of Indiana, Illinois, and Kentucky. The farthest west they had traveled was St. Louis. They just didn't see the need to travel much outside of Indiana, when everything they wanted or needed was right there—except that wasn't how Nash felt. Maybe it was the first few years of his life, but he loved experiencing new things. Yes, he loved his hometown and the people in it. He loved the way folks greeted him at the grocery store, and the way family was the most important thing. He loved that loyalty was expected among friends, and he could always count on his buddies to help him out of trouble, or get him into trouble, depending on the day. But he started getting the itch to attend the Academy when he learned about his dad, and he hadn't been able to shake it since.

After his dad died, Nash's mom was so heartbroken; she found it painful to talk about him very much. But Nash and Mason needed a safe space to grieve, and their mom tried to give it to them. She made sure they had pictures of their dad all over the house and in their bedrooms. She would participate in their "Remember when dad . . . " ritual and remind them of fun family vacations or silly games their dad used to play with them when they were young. Sometimes she would tell stories of how excited he was to be a father, or how handsome she thought he was when they began dating after college. But she hardly shared anything about his military experience. She often remarked on how his dad didn't bring work home. Nash wondered if she didn't know very much about what his father's day-to-day life in the military was really like. And although Nash knew that his dad went to the Academy and then served in the military, he didn't really understand what any of that entailed. His mom had tried to tell Nash how seriously he took his duty, his oath to his nation, but none of it made much sense to a kid. With each passing day at the Academy, Nash felt like his understanding was growing deeper.

Nash had vague memories of wrestling around in the backyard with his dad, throwing a football, listening to a bedtime story, or watching cartoons with him—their favorite was SpongeBob. Other than that, Nash had lost his memories, which scared him more than the day he learned his father was dead. Sometimes Nash didn't know if he was only doing this—going to the Academy, putting up with all this—because of his dad. But if he was only doing it for someone else, the memory of someone else, was he really capable of doing it at all? Was knowing that his dad went here enough to sustain him for four more years?

On the day of the Chem GR, Nash walked around in a sort of inescapable funk. By the end of the week, he was beat. It was like he was filled up with all the stress and tension he could stomach, and by Friday he was ready to throw in the towel. Those were usually the moments when Smokey found Nash doing something wrong. That dude seemed to be everywhere Nash went. He could not get away from the voice that shook Nash to his very core. The kick straight to the balls of Nash's joy came as soon as he entered the front door of the dorms.

"CADET KAPLAN! YOU FAILED YOUR ROOM INSPECTION! I EXPECT YOUR ROOM READY FOR REINSPECTION IN TWENTY MINUTES!"

"YES, SIR!" Nash responded with one of the seven basic responses before sprinting away to see what damage Smokey had done.

He wasn't disappointed. Smokey had tossed everything he could lay his hands on. It was like a war had been waged in the room, a war against the mattresses, blankets, clothes, and school supplies that the occupants had foolishly left unguarded. *No, not a war*, Nash thought, *a category-five hurricane had come through*. Shit was everywhere.

This was the last thing Nash wanted to deal with before the weekend. A failed room inspection undoubtedly meant that any hope of leaving the base on Saturday wasn't going to come to fruition. It all depended on what sort of mood Smokey would be in when he came back to inspect. Based on historical evidence, Nash was not hopeful about a positive outcome.

He started first with their desk supplies. Smokey had knocked everything off their desks: books, papers, pens, pencils, water bottles, staplers, calendars. Whatever he could get his hands on was tossed carelessly on the floor. Nash started making sense of what stuff was his and what was Jake's.

As he reached under Jake's desk to grab an errant water bottle, the label began to peel off in his grip. Before Nash completely pulled it off and crumpled it up for the trash, he noticed there was writing all over it, tiny, neatly formed letters, handwritten all over a smallish square of paper and placed perfectly underneath the water bottle's original label. Nash folded the label back around the side of the water bottle and looked through the clear plastic on the other side. He could read the chemical reaction formulas perfectly through the other side of the bottle—the bottle Jake carried around with him now that they weren't made to wear basic training CamelBaks.

Nash set the bottle down on Jake's desk and backed away from it like it was a grenade. Maybe it wasn't what he thought it was, right? Maybe Jake hadn't taken it to class. But Nash's stomach began to churn. Maybe he changed his mind about cheating on the damn GR. Maybe.

Nash finished righting the rest of the room just as Jake walked in. "Holy shit! Smokey strikes again, huh? Man, that guy is a bastard."

"Yeah, he's coming back in about ten minutes to re-inspect." Nash replied to Jake without turning around to look at him. He kept folding the T-shirts into neat squares and placing them back in their drawers.

"You want some tape for those?" Jake asked Nash, nodding at the T-shirts he was folding. A trick they had learned was to tape up the corners to keep them within the right measurements, and to keep them from sliding around when the drawer was pulled open or pushed closed. There was a skill to it because if the tape was visible, the upperclassmen would ransack your room even harder than they did before. They didn't like shortcuts unless they were the ones taking them.

"No, that's all right. We can redo them this

weekend, when we're stuck in here." Nash just wanted to get the room ready and get away.

"C'mon, dude. Let me slap some tape on those fuckers so they don't dance all over the fucking place. You know Smokey's going to get his balls in a wad if this place isn't spic and fucking span." Jake turned around to get the tape from his desk and saw the water bottle sitting there on top of his calendar.

Nash watched as he slowly reached for it and turned back toward him.

"Do you know if Smokey saw this?" Without waiting for Nash to answer, Jake continued, "Of course he didn't or he'd be up my ass right now."

Nash kept his eyes on Jake as he pushed the drawer in slowly and stood up. "Did you use it?" He didn't have to explain to Jake that he was talking about the cheat sheet under the label. They both knew exactly what he was referring to, and it wasn't the water inside.

Jake grinned at Nash like they were

conspirators, in this together. "C'mon, dude. You know I don't care about this shit enough to cheat. I had a momentary brain lapse last night because I didn't get any sleep. I had the idea to jot down a couple formulas in case that dick Maynard tried to pull a fast one on me and test me on something outside the study guide. Turns out, he didn't, so I didn't even need my GR tool."

"I looked at the formulas, Jake. They were from the study guide. Stuff you would definitely need for the GR." Nash's heart was beating fast. He knew this wasn't going to end like he had hoped, with Jake not taking the water bottle to class, not using the cheat sheet, not doing any of it.

Jake's grin left his face. "You're right, Kap. But I really didn't use it. I left it in my backpack the whole time."

Nash swallowed hard and asked, "Are you going to tell Maynard you had it?"

"Of course! Right after I call my pops and tell

him. While I'm at it, why don't I let him know how the Audi got that scratch on the back panel? Or let my mom know where those beers wandered off to last Easter weekend? I might as well call the Admissions Office and tell them how many times I really smoked weed last summer." Jake rolled his eyes at Nash in disgust. "Give me a fuckin' break, Nash. I'm not telling Maynard shit. I didn't do anything to tell him about, anyway. C'mon, let's just clean up this shit before Smokey gets back up here." Jake began placing things in their wall lockers.

After a few frozen seconds, Nash joined him in silence.

CHAPTER 11

Nash didn't sleep all night thinking about what to do. Fuckin' Jake. Fuckin' oath. Nash felt like he was going to eat a shit sandwich no matter what. If he pushed Jake to turn himself in, then what? Hell, he could lose all of his friends. The last guy people wanted to hang out with was the guy who was going to try to convince them to "do the right thing." That guy was a buzzkill. Nobody liked that guy, right? Nash didn't even like that guy. But the alternative was to turn Jake in himself, and Nash didn't think he could do it, no matter what oath he took.

There was another choice: do nothing. Ignore

all of it. Pretend like it never happened. Pretend like he didn't see the cheat sheet. Pretend like Jake didn't know that Nash found it. Pretend like Jake didn't cheat, which they both knew he did. Pretend like the oath was bullshit. Pretend like Nash was the kind of guy to take an oath and not mean it. Was he? He tossed and turned all night with those thoughts running through his brain.

In the morning, Nash pretended to still be asleep when Jake went off to boxing practice. Nash couldn't deal with him right now, not before he figured out what to do next. He needed to think. He jumped down from his bunk and headed to the bathroom to shave and brush his teeth. Saturday mornings were much more leisurely than the weekdays. They were able to sleep in until zero-six forty-five, because breakfast was served until zero-seven on the weekends. *Yep*, Nash thought sarcastically, *definitely living the good life here.* But he also learned to appreciate the extra hour of sleep he was able to get on the weekends. And with all the stuff they had to get done during the day, he couldn't imagine sleeping in until noon like he sometimes used to back home. Besides, everybody else was up doing stuff, too. Every room Nash walked past had a Doolie ironing his uniform, refolding T-shirts and underwear into their approved dimensions, or studying for some class. It was like a little beehive with all the drones buzzing around doing their tasks.

After he finished his morning ritual of shaving the peach fuzz off his face, he quickly dressed in his Air Force Blues and hurried off to chow. During the first days of basic, Nash struggled to get his uniform on in the five minutes they were allowed to dress. His shirt was always wrinkled and his nametag was usually crooked. On the bottom half, his belt was never in line with his fly like it was supposed to be, and he would have gleefully hunted down and killed the person who invented the shirt garter if given the chance. The garter was an elastic band that was supposed to clip on to the bottom of his uniform shirt and the top of his black grandpa socks. It was used to create a snug appearance to the front and back of the tucked-in shirt. The problem was, it had to be pulled so tight in order to hold the shirt into place that sometimes one or the other of the clips would lose their grip and snap off like a giant rubber band headed straight for the backs of Nash's legs. Now, the garter snapping was the absolute last thing Nash worried about. He had mastered the garter and moved onto much higher level drama—like whether or not to rat out his friend for cheating.

The weekend went on like Nash wasn't in a moral dilemma. Even though his weekend pass was revoked, Nash was still allowed to attend the Saturday afternoon football game. In fact, all Doolies had to attend, whether they wanted to or not.

Academy football games were an experience all by themselves. The entire student body had to attend each home game, and the Doolies used them as an opportunity to relax, eat too many hotdogs, and walk around like regular college freshmen without fear of being "trained" by the upperclassmen. Nash usually enjoyed himself at these games; there was so much history and tradition at each one. Before the game started, the student body would march onto the field, thousands of them walking on before heading into the stands. Then, the Wings of Blue would parachute down with an American flag strapped to one of their ankles. They would glide down to earth like feathers flying back and forth, landing like blue puffs of cotton, light as air. Next year, Nash could apply to become a member of the parachute team, and he could be the one gliding down from the heavens. During half-time, the Falconers, usually juniors or seniors, would show off their trained birds, swooping over the members of the audience to land on the wrists of their Academy cadet. At each touchdown, the Doolies would empty their seats, pouring onto the field to join the Superintendent, a four-star general, outside the end zone to do a push-up for each point on the scoreboard.

Nash really enjoyed attending the games during football season. They were a release from the stressors of everyday life at the Academy. He could kick back and check out the girls, or call his brother and mom to catch up. He could wander around the stands and meet his classmates' families, or just watch how happy people were to see their sons and daughters, brothers and sisters. It reminded Nash of games in his hometown, and he felt like it was a little bit of Clarksville right there between the mountains.

But this Saturday was different. Nash had to decide what to do about Jake, and he didn't know to whom he could talk about it. He wasn't ready to talk to Greene and Sully either, because as soon as he told them, they would also be obligated to confront Jake, and possibly turn him in for cheating. Instead, Nash decided to call Mason. Even though

Mason was his younger brother, he trusted his advice. Mason had a level head on his shoulders, and Nash felt like Mason would be able to talk him through how to think about this.

"Hello, buttface! How the heck are ya?" Mason's voice sounded excited.

Nash smiled at the sound of him on the other end. "I'm good, little brother. How's Mom?"

"She's good. She's at work today, but she'll be home around five. What's going on there? You having a band party?" Nash realized Mason could hear the Academy band playing through the phone. "I'm looking for you on TV. They're televising the game on CBS!"

"I don't think you'll find me, little brother. I'm in a sea of blue-clad Smurfs. But I'll look for the cameras and try to stick my mug out there just in case." Nash half-heartedly chuckled.

"I'm glad you called. I gotta tell you about the date I had with Jill last night—" Mason started, but Nash interrupted him.

"Hold on, let me get somewhere quieter. I'm trying to get through this crowd . . . " When Mason had answered his call, Nash had almost made it to underneath the top row bleachers where the noise was less intense. "There, how's that?"

"Yeah, I can hear you much better now. Dude! Okay, so we went to see some chick flick she liked and as we were leaving the theater we bumped into Erica . . . " As Mason continued on with the details of his run-in with his ex-girlfriend, Nash closed his eyes and wished they were sitting together at the kitchen table. No, better yet, lying down in the backyard under the shade tree. He felt such a wave of homesickness that he almost couldn't breathe. He wanted so badly to have the problem of being on a date and running into an ex. Nash never thought that would be something to envy, but here he was jealous of his little brother's drama. He continued to listen to Mason's voice finish the tale.

After a few more minutes of working through Mason's issues of having too many girls to pick from, Nash finally injected, "I need to talk to you about a pretend." A *pretend* was their word when they wanted to discuss hypothetical situations, usually situations that had already happened, but they weren't yet ready to admit it to the universe—like the time Mason wanted to pretend he had backed the family car up into the lake behind their house. "Pretend the car's back wheels are stuck in the lake, Nash. What would you do?" Now, it was Nash's turn to pretend with Mason.

"Okay, big brother, let me have it. Did you get someone pregnant?"

Nash guffawed at that, not expecting his brother to ever ask him that question, and definitely not expecting him to think that was a possibility for them at the Academy with all the leisure time they were given.

"No, nothing like that, Mase, geez! Pretend a buddy did something against the rules, and you knew about it."

"What am I pretending he did? I mean, is this

like, going to the cops for a murder, or for having a beer under the bleachers kind of stuff?"

"Pretend he cheated on a big test." Nash sighed deeply and waited for his brother to respond. Mason didn't say anything for what felt like five minutes, but was probably more like a few seconds.

"Okay . . . " Mason replied. "Then what, Nash?"

"Well, that's it. He cheated and you know about it. Would you turn him in? I mean, if you made a promise that you would turn someone in for doing that—for cheating." Nash finished hurriedly and waited anxiously for Mason's reply.

"I think I'm missing something here, Nash. Hasn't anyone ever cheated before? I mean, I cheated on my Spanish quiz last year. Are you gonna go to Señora Garza and tell on me?"

Mason was trying to be funny, but he was really getting on Nash's nerves.

"Damn it, this is a serious pretend, Mase." Nash realized how ridiculous he sounded. "And if I did know that someone cheated, I would be breaking a promise—if I didn't turn him in—it's not like back home. I don't think they play around with that stuff. It's not some high school Spanish quiz. It's the kind of stuff Mom used to say about Dad—you know, how he believed in the oath he took—it's like that, I think. I don't know. I don't know what I'm saying right now."

There was a long silence on the other end before Mason replied, "Okay, look, I know you wouldn't rat out a friend, Nash. There's got to be another choice, right?"

"Yeah, there are options: social leper or lying dirtbag. Not the best choices." Nash said sarcastically. "Look, I gotta get back. Someone will bust my balls if I don't show up for some of the game. Tell Mom I called and I'll call her back tomorrow, if I can, okay?" Nash was annoyed by his brother; for what reason, he couldn't quite put into words. It was as if he was irritated because Mason didn't understand. But then, how could he? He hadn't sworn to uphold any code. He hadn't made a promise in front of all the other Doolies not to lie, steal, cheat, or tolerate anyone among them who did. Mason still lived in the world where loyalty was king, and buddies didn't rat each other out. What would Mason think if Nash turned in Jake? Would he be disappointed in him? The phone call was supposed to make things better, but had the opposite effect.

After the game, Nash planned to spend the rest of the day in McDermott Library working on his English essay and avoiding Jake until he was sure he'd left for winter break. Nash still wasn't ready to confront him.

In the library, there was a spot near the military history section where Nash liked to plant himself with his computer, headphones, and solitude to get down to business. Being surrounded by people telling him what to do all the time really made a guy appreciate being left the hell alone. If only he could be alone behind the wheel of his truck, and not have to decide whether or not to rat out his buddy, nearly all would be right with the world.

Even though Nash was supposed to be researching for his class essay, he couldn't concentrate on the matter at hand. He sat there in front of a largely blank screen, with stacks of books scattered around the table he'd commandeered. That's how Captain Waters found him when she turned down the War of the Confederacy aisle.

"Hello, Cadet Kaplan. Enjoying your Saturday?" She greeted him with genuine interest in her voice.

Maybe for that reason, or maybe because she seemed to truly believe in the things she taught in class, that Nash gave an honest response. "Not really, ma'am."

Captain Waters moved closer to the table Nash occupied between the stacks of long-dead generals, her brows furrowed together in concern. "What's going on, Kaplan? Is there something I can help you with?"

"I don't know, really," Nash continued, "I've been thinking about the honor code, and maybe you could clear up a few things for me . . . if I were to give you a hypothetical situation . . . could you do that, or not?"

"Okay . . . " Captain Waters sat down across from Nash.

"What part of the honor code do you think causes cadets the most trouble? I mean, if you had to choose one part of it that maybe tripped people up the most—what would it be, do you think?"

"Well, it really depends on the person's experiences, but if I were made to choose," she raised one of her eyebrows at him, "I'd have to say toleration."

"Why do you think that is? Again, if you were made to guess." Nash gave her a half-smile in response to her eyebrow lift.

"Well, I think most folks are brought up that 'snitches get stitches'—it doesn't rhyme for nothing," she laughed at her own joke. "And we think that telling on a friend is disloyal. When I teach the honor code lessons, I'm aware of the cultural shift I'm encouraging—this shift from thinking of it as disloyal to thinking of it as loving."

"Whoa—I definitely don't know if I've made that shift to *loving*. How could it be loving to snitch on a buddy?" Nash sighed and looked away at nothing.

"I'm not sure you understand the toleration part of the code, Cadet Kaplan. It isn't to encourage snitching, it's to encourage accountability." Captain Waters sat back in her seat and waited for her words to sink in a bit. She began again, "Lots of schools have honor codes, but the Academy's code requires other students to not tolerate honor violations. And it's not because we want you all to tattle on each other. It's because we want you to encourage each other to do the right thing. Who better to convince someone to come clean than another cadet?"

Nash looked back at her, holding eye contact

for a few seconds before dropping his gaze. "I'd never thought of it that way before. So the goal is to get us to convince each other to do the right thing? Hypothetically?"

"Yes. We're looking to develop solid character, not to develop rats. The ultimate goal is to create a community that, as a whole, does not tolerate misconduct. The code should lift each of us to be our best self. If someone breaks the code, then he or she should report it. If the individual chooses not to, it is only then that another cadet should step in for him or her. Anything else would not be compatible with what we are looking for in the Air Force."

"But what happens if he doesn't turn himself in, and someone else has to do it? I don't think that person is going to get a pat on the back from everyone else." Nash knew if he ratted on Jake he would be called a traitor. If Waters tried to convince him otherwise, she was full of shit.

Captain Waters's tone was serious, "Cadet

Kaplan, I'm an Academy grad. I know what it's like. And you're right. Most likely, the person who turns in someone else would be distrusted by some—or more than some. But he would know what he was made of." The confused look on Nash's face made Captain Waters smile a little. She continued, "Cadet Kaplan, my hope is that you would do the right thing. If that time ever comes," Captain Waters said as she pushed her chair back from the table and stood up to leave.

Nash's eyes stared blankly at the empty computer screen. *That was the problem, wasn't it?* Nash thought. *What was the right thing to do?* Just then, Nash remembered Jake's own advice about the code, *"The way I think about it, every single person will have taken this oath just like us. Every single one of these sonsabitches is promising not to lie, or fuckin' cheat, or steal shit. So if one of them does, they've already broke their promise, right? So fuck 'em. They don't deserve any loyalty after that."*

Nash wondered if Jake remembered those words.

The next day, Nash attended his regular church service at the Academy chapel. Nash's mom was one of those deep believers, and it made her feel good if Nash soaked up some faith on Sundays. So he partly did it for her, but he did it for himself, too. This Sunday he was hoping some message might even come to him about what to do about Jake.

As usual, as Nash approached the chapel he was in awe of the beauty of the place. From the outside, it represented modernist architecture from the 1960s, as its seventeen spires jutted toward the heavens in sharp angles. Nash knew more about the construction of the chapel than he did about any other building on campus—hell, any other building in the world. Every cadet memorized the dimensions of the structure and could recite them on command. Nash had to recite the information more than once during his many training sessions with the upperclassmen: "Sir, the Cadet Chapel is one hundred and fifty feet high, two hundred eighty feet long, and eighty-four feet wide. It was constructed in 1962 with a design by Walter Netsch. The chapel is made up of one hundred identical steel triangles, each seventy-five feet long. The triangles are spaced twelve inches apart with one-inch-thick stained glass between." If a Doolie was able to state that information verbatim, he might escape further training in the form of push-ups. Even though Nash had done his share of push-ups for the chapel, it didn't sour the beauty of the place for him.

When he entered through the chapel doors, a kaleidoscope of colors enveloped him as the sun streamed through the stained glass. He picked a seat near the rear of the church, and watched as the congregation settled inside. The congregation wasn't all that different from Clarksville First United Church's—lots of families from the community, many, Nash guessed, had been attending the church fairly regularly by the way they were greeted with hearty handshakes and hugs. Where things were a little different was the multitude of college kids in military uniforms crammed into the pews.

Nash wouldn't be able to swing a cat by the tail without hitting a cadet during Sunday service. There were a lot of instructors at the services, too. Most of them worked weekend shifts on campus, so this was an opportunity to attend service and see who was also into Jesus, or, at least, into being at the chapel so they didn't have to do Sunday details—maybe a mixture of both. But today's service was extra special because it was the last one before winter break. The cadets were buzzing with anticipatory energy. Many of them were headed home to visit family for the next two weeks, and Nash was no exception. His plane was taking off in less than four hours.

Church service at the Academy wasn't unlike Sunday service back home, either. There were hymns sung to kick off the sermon, and the pastor could be counted on to deliver a message about faith, perseverance, strength or joy in the face of life's difficulties. But this Sunday, the sermon didn't help Nash come to any decisions with its message of David taking down Goliath. For one, Nash didn't see himself as David, the scrawny sheepherder kid, and Jake wasn't a behemoth giant ready to crush anything or anyone who came into his path. Besides, Nash definitely didn't feel brave like David. David volunteered to fight this ginormous asshole with only a slingshot, and Nash had been avoiding even seeing Jake for the last twenty-four hours. If anything, the service made Nash feel worse, not better. He just wanted to get out of there and get on a plane home.

After the service ended, Nash made his way outside to a barrage of Colorado sunshine and he had to close his eyes after the cave-like atmosphere of the Academy's famous chapel. It took several seconds for his eyes to adjust to the brightness waiting for him, and he nearly ran over Captain Waters.

"So sorry, ma'am!" he blurted as he tried to side-step and avoid smashing into her. Instead, he scuffed the toe of her shiny black shoes. *Shit.*

"It's okay, Cadet Kaplan. It seems like you can't escape me this weekend. Anymore hypotheticals you need help working through?" she asked.

No escape from the honor lesson instructor. *Subtle*, Nash thought to the universe. *Really subtle.*

"No, ma'am. I'm still working through the last one."

"Don't wait too long, Cadet Kaplan. Bad predicaments don't always disappear with time. Sometimes they grow bigger—like Goliath!"

Captain Waters seemed pleased she was able to tie in the sermon reference.

"Yes, ma'am."

Shit. Nash was afraid she had a point. The conversation with Jake wasn't going to get easier the longer he put it off. But he was glad for the chance to get away and clear his head. He'd talk to Jake when the break was over.

CHAPTER 14

Nash had been home for less than twenty-four hours. The trip back from Colorado was a long one, and he was happy to be in his house, in his bed, asleep. Well, not exactly asleep, but able to go back to sleep if he wanted to—but he couldn't. His body had gotten used to getting up before the sunrise, and he woke up without any alarm. *Shit.* Even his body was militarized now. Maybe that's what he deserved, never to be allowed to sleep past zero-five hundred again.

It was a long trip from Colorado to Indiana; he had to switch planes once, and the second plane was late arriving at the airport. All the passengers had to wait for a few hours before they could continue to Indiana. And the entire time he was waiting, Nash kept thinking about how he needed to talk to Jake.

Nash threw back the covers and headed to the kitchen for a sunrise breakfast. He needed coffee. He had never been a big coffee fan before the Academy, but he had chosen it as a safer alternative to the Monster drinks that other Doolies were always pounding. He had read about the effects of that shit, and it was like poison. He would stick with a cup of coffee a day, thank you very much.

As he made his way into the kitchen, he was surprised to see the light already on under the swinging door. As he pushed the door open, he was greeted by the sight of his mom sitting at the kitchen table, sipping on a cup of coffee and reading the newspaper.

"Morning, Mom," he grumbled, his lips grudgingly moving to allow the words through.

"Good morning, hon! What are you doing up

so early? I thought you'd be sleeping like the dead until this afternoon!"

"Me, too, but I guess my body's used to the Academy schedule."

"Well, can I make you some bacon and eggs? It will only take a minute." She was already folding up the newspaper.

"Thanks, Mom. That sounds delicious," Nash mumbled.

Nash's mom pushed her chair back from the table and started getting the bacon and eggs from the fridge. Nash zombied over to the coffee pot and began pouring some into a mug.

"Drinking coffee now?" His mom was surprised. "Well, I guess my boy is now a man," she joked.

"Yep, I've made it—finally." They laughed together as the bacon popped over the stove's flames.

Nash wrapped his hands around the warmth of the mug, and stared off into the kitchen's sunny floor tiles. He didn't notice his mom watching him carefully.

"So, how are things going, Nash? Are you eating enough? You've lost so much weight! But you look great!" His mom was quick to include a compliment.

Nash smiled a lopsided grin and shrugged his shoulders. "Things are different there than I expected."

"Really? Like what? You watched so many You-Tube videos about the place that I can't imagine you didn't expect most of it." Nash's mom tilted her head and flipped the bacon over.

Nash joined his mom at the counter and began cracking open eggs into a bowl. "Like classes. They're kicking everybody's butt! The workload is really crazy."

"Oh, I bet. But you've always been a good student, Nash. You know how to study, and how to manage your time." His mom put a hand on his cheek for a second before turning back to the bacon in the skillet.

"Yeah, and I'm doing that, but it's just so much of everything. We take like twenty credit hours, Mom. That's insane!" Nash began whipping the eggs together in preparation for the waiting hot skillet.

"That's a lot of hours, son. Are you doing okay?" she asked, concerned.

"I'm doing better than some guys, but worse than others. We're all sort of in it together, and we do try to help each other out."

"How's Jake doing? That's your roommate's name, right? I imagine with his experience with these types of schools, he's probably got a few tricks up his sleeve." Nash saw his mom's genuine smile as she looked up at him.

"Yeah. Yeah, he does. Too many tricks." Nash mumbled.

"What's that, honey? I didn't hear you." The

bacon was going nuts in the skillet, and his mom had turned on the exhaust fan over the stove.

"Nothin', Mom. Just that Jake is helping me out. For sure."

Nash could tell his mom knew something was bothering him, but he didn't know if he could tell his mom the truth right now. He didn't know if he could tell her he was thinking of ratting out his friend. Was he thinking of that? He didn't even know himself.

Nash's mom turned off the flames under the bacon, then the eggs.

"Grab a plate, kid."

Nash walked over to the cupboard and got down one of the bright red dishes. *They don't have these in the chow hall,* he thought. *They really should have them, though.* They were cheery.

"I sure have missed home, Mom," he said as he handed her the plate and she began to load it with fluffy eggs and crisp bacon. The smell filled the kitchen, and Nash almost felt relaxed for the first time since he stepped off the plane.

"What the heck is everyone doing up so early?" Mason pushed through the swinging door, still rubbing his eyes awake. His cowlick was in full effect.

"What do you mean, baby brother? This is the time when the adults get up nowadays. You youngins stay in bed, laze about, wait for the grown folks to do all the work," Nash teased.

"Is that right? Did Mommy make your breakfast for you?" Mason jabbed an elbow at Nash, making him splash coffee on the kitchen tiles.

"Jerk! Yes, my mommy made me breakfast. She loves me best. Give me that towel, monkey boy."

Mason threw the kitchen towel hard at Nash's face. Nash caught it with a grin, and dropped it at his feet to soak up the spilled mess.

"Boys, that's enough. I love you both the same. Do you want Mommy to make you some breakfast, Masie?" She joined in the teasing with her sons.

"Yes, please," Mason sing-songed, and jabbed at

Nash again. Nash put down the coffee cup and the two began headlocking and lightly punching each other in the kitchen.

"That's enough! Get out of my kitchen! If you want to wrestle, go outside," their mom commanded.

Nash laughed with Mason and they sat down together at the table while their mom hummed a tune.

After breakfast, all Nash wanted to do was get behind the wheel of his truck and drive. In Clarksville, there were country roads for miles, and a full tank of gas could entertain Nash for an entire day. He didn't intend to be gone all day; he had lunch plans with Jimmy and some other buddies from high school, but he did want to get away and think for a while.

Should Nash call Jake? Was this something to

do over the phone? Nash ruled that out right away. He knew he couldn't have this discussion with Jake over the phone. He would have to wait until they were face to face, which made Nash even more nervous. How was he supposed to start a conversation like this anyway?

Hey, Jake, I know we're friends and all, but we both know you cheated on the GR. Why don't you turn yourself in, buddy, so I don't have to do it? That sounded ridiculous inside Nash's head, so he could only assume how stupid it would sound out loud.

Maybe Nash wouldn't have to confront Jake. Maybe Jake was in Texas right now gathering enough courage to tell his parents, and then they would all do a conference call with the honor board so Jake could come clean. *Yeah right.*

It didn't seem like time was going to give him the answer he wanted. No matter which way he sliced the problem, it wasn't going to change: Jake had cheated, and Nash knew about it. Nash's promise to uphold the honor oath either meant something, or it didn't. Only Nash could figure that out for himself. But he decided he wasn't going to let this ruin any more of his time at home. He was determined to have some fun and relax so he could get back ready to tackle the rest of Doolie year.

After driving around for a while, Nash met his buddies for lunch at Diane's Café, one of the local haunts they used to frequent in high school. Jimmy and the rest of the crew were waiting for him in a corner booth.

"Hey! There he is, Mr. Air Force!" Jimmy greeted him loudly, and the rest of the guys whistled and clapped. The other customers turned to see why all the commotion. *Assholes*, Nash thought with a smile.

"All right, all right. Enough from you jackals," Nash said in his most military-tone voice.

Jimmy stood up and gave Nash a rib-crushing

bear hug, lifting him off the ground and spinning and bouncing him around like a doll. "Welcome home, cousin!" he boomed.

"Th-thanks, I th-think," Nash stammered out between bounces.

The guys settled down into the booth, and they joked and laughed with each other all through their lunch of chicken fried steaks and meatloaf. Nash had definitely missed Diane's. He'd put back on that weight his mom noticed he'd lost in no time.

"So what are you doing for the rest of the day, Nash? You hanging out with us, or what, bigshot?" Trent, friends with Nash since second grade, asked from across the table as lunch was winding down and they were paying their checks.

"My plans are all about you delinquents. I'm yours until six. Mom has dinner planned for me, and you know she'll kill me if I'm late. But that gives us a few hours. What do you want to do? Head out to the lake?" Nash loved to fish with his friends, or hang out on the pier.

"Hell no! It's cold as a witch's tit out there," one of the guys whined.

Jimmy jumped in, "We can build a fire, princess. Nash is home and he wants to see the lake. Let's do it. But let's swing by Popper's and grab some beers first," Jimmy suggested.

One of the guys piped up, "Can I ride with you, Nash? I'm squished in Jimmy's ride. They always make me sit in the middle."

"It's because of your tiny bones," Jimmy teased their little friend.

"Forget you, fatty. Don't be jealous because I can still button my pants after I eat, and your *wife* is making you plump!" Nash loved how his friends could give as good as they got. Jake would like them, Nash decided before quickly casting that thought to the side. Nash missed this for sure. He missed the easy way they all got along. He missed being around people who knew him so well, knew everything about him, and shared the same ideas about how friendship worked.

One time in high school, they had been at a party at an old farmhouse. There were lots of kids, lots of beer, and eventually, lots of yelling from the owner when he showed up to find some wrecked stall doors and broken bottles from the party. Because Nash lived in a town without strangers, the owner knew the twenty or so kids on sight, or more importantly, he knew their parents. The owner didn't bother to ask them where they got the beer or whose party it was—neither question would have garnered straight answers anyway. No one would have talked. Rather than call the cops, he called their parents and made the kids—Nash included—pay for the damage. And they all did, some even helping the others to come up with the money.

But what Nash remembered most weren't the consequences each of them faced at home. His mom was less than pleased with Nash's being at the party, and she took away his truck for a month, not to mention the extra shifts he had to pull at the Golf and Games to pay for the damages. His life pretty much sucked for a long time after that. Nash's mom was livid, but she was tame compared to what Nash could have lost. His dream of attending the Academy could have quickly ended that night if the owner had called the police.

Somehow, the consequences now seemed even steeper. Disenrollment from the Academy wasn't a few extra shifts at the Golf and Games. If Jake's parents found out, what would they do? Jake's dad was a retired *general*, for fuck's sake. Nash couldn't imagine breaking that news to him if he were Jake. Nash wanted to talk to his buddies about what happened at school, but he wasn't sure they would understand the position he was in, like Mason hadn't. Like so many times before, Nash wished his dad were still alive. He had a feeling he would understand.

"You ready to head out?" Jimmy nudged Nash out of his daydreams.

"Yep, let's go."

The rest of the afternoon was spent shooting the shit around the fire pit. His buddies threw back Miller Lites and smoked weed while Nash kept waving off the offers to partake.

"Get that shit away from me, dude." Nash stretched out his legs and leaned back, away from Jimmy's outstretched hand with the joint in it.

"Shit, man. I forgot. Sorry about that. Do you hate it? Not being able to do what you want?" Jimmy asked.

Trent, another friend since elementary school, added, "I couldn't do it, for real. All those bastards screaming in my face? I'd have to go off on somebody."

"We know it doesn't take much to push you over the edge of crazy, T," Nash joked.

"Remember when Trent punched that dude from Notre Dame High and broke his jaw? That *was* crazy! All because he bumped into Tracy during the festival and didn't apologize."

"Hey, man, I was drinking back then . . . and that guy was an asshole who had that broken jaw coming to him for a long time. Guess what, though? He's working at the plant now, third shift. I see him in the parking lot sometimes after I've clocked out. He never says hi though . . . unfriendly type." The guys chuckled.

"Seriously, Nash, how are you doing it, man?" Jimmy asked.

"You know, I'm a lover not a fighter," Nash smiled as the rest of them groaned and rolled their eyes. "And I'm not a pothead like you, Jimmy." Jimmy pretended to salute him with his middle finger as Nash laughed. "It's not been as hard as I thought it was going to be—getting used to having someone tell you what to do every minute of every day isn't the hardest part. The hardest part seems to be when no one tells you what to do, and you have to figure it out on your own." Nash wished someone would tell him how to handle his situation with Jake. He couldn't believe he actually missed the days of basic training when he didn't have to think so much. He shook himself out of his daydream. "I miss being here, miss hanging out with you guys. I'm still trying to get used to the change in rules there. They expect different things from me . . . "

They all sat silently for a while, each one in his own thoughts of how life had changed in the months since they graduated high school.

"Well, thanks for killing my buzz, man." Jimmy was the first to speak. "Welcome home, buddy! It's great having you around again!" Nash couldn't kill Jimmy's buzz if he tried, and he knew Jimmy was joking. But it struck a nerve anyway.

"You're welcome." Nash shot back before quickly coming to his feet. "It's late, and Mom will not be happy if I'm late tonight. I'll catch up with you all tomorrow?" Nash stepped back and started heading back toward his truck. "Trent, you able to drive all these delinquents back home since me and you are the only respectable folks in the group who don't get drunk in the middle of the afternoon?"

"Yeah, I got all these bastards. Call me tomorrow," he hollered after Nash.

Nash waved back as he climbed into the cab of his truck and fired up the engine. As he drove off, he looked in his rearview mirror, watching his friends—his family—as they stayed behind, growing smaller and smaller as he drove away.

CHAPTER 15

Dinner was one of Nash's favorites: pork chops, corn on the cob, creamy mashed potatoes with lots of butter and gravy, and homemade apple pie. His mom was definitely trying to put some weight back on him before he returned to Colorado. She cooked Nash's favorites for the entire two weeks he was home.

The rest of his visit home went much like the first few days. Nash woke early every morning, had coffee with his mom, drove around the country roads, went for a run, and spent the rest of the day visiting family and friends, catching up with the happenings of their lives, and not really sharing too much about how his own had changed. He felt strangely isolated in his own dilemma.

In his final couple days home, Nash had told his mom what he was struggling with at school. Once again, Nash didn't expect what happened next.

"Nash, I know I don't talk about your dad much—at all really," his mom began. "And I'm sorry. It hurts to think of him sometimes. You kids know that he was a man of honor. He really did live by a code, and that meant everything to him." She grasped Nash's hand between her own as they sat on the front porch swing, rocking back and forth and enjoying the unpredictably mild temperatures of the Indiana weather. "Now, don't get me wrong. Your dad wasn't perfect, but I could count on him to keep his word. You remind me so much of him." Her eyes were glistening, the tears almost spilling over as she smiled at Nash. "Stay right there," she continued. "I think it's time to give you something." She got up from the swing and went inside the house; the slam of the screen door followed her.

Nash stayed on the swing, rocking back and forth as he gazed out over the front yard. It was so quiet he could hear the wind rustling over the straw-grass. When she returned, she held a blue folder in her hands. She sat down and slid it across the table to Nash. "Open it," she directed.

Nash's hand trembled as his fingertips glided across the Air Force seal embossed on the front of the folder. He felt the ridges pressed down in gold. Then he opened the folder and saw his father's name at the top of the official-looking page. Also at the top was a gold cross with an eagle splayed across the middle. Wrapped around the cross was a green wreath. Nash read the document to himself.

THE UNITED STATES OF AMERICA. TO ALL WHO SHALL SEE THESE PRESENTS, GREETING: THIS IS TO CERTIFY THAT THE PRESIDENT OF THE UNITED STATES HAS AWARDED THE AIR FORCE CROSS TO MAJOR DAVIS T. KAPLAN.

Nash's throat immediately choked up, but he continued reading about his father's *extraordinary heroism in southern Afghanistan on 23 March 2009.* The date his father died was right there on the page. So much of what Nash didn't know about that day was neatly typed and laying between his hands. *Major Kaplan volunteered to lead a strike package against a high-value target after another F-15E had been shot down.* Nash gulped hard to stop the sob that formed in his throat. His dad had known the dangers he was facing and he flew the mission anyway. Nash just shook his head in amazement and kept reading about how his father *eradicated the enemy with superb airmanship*, and how *because of Major Kaplan's heroism and integrity in upholding an oath to support and defend, he enabled the rescue of another downed crew before losing his own life to enemy fire.* Nash didn't even feel the tears coming down his cheeks. He didn't know he was crying until he felt his mom's hand brush across his face.

He looked up from the folder and saw the tears on her cheeks, too.

She whispered, "He would be so proud to see what you're doing now, Nash. He would love it so much."

CHAPTER 16

When Nash returned from winter break, Jake was in their room, unpacking. They hadn't seen each other for two weeks. Their greeting was a little awkward and tense, like strangers.

"So, how was your break?" Jake spoke first. "Did you get laid?"

Nash shook his head, annoyed that Jake was trying to act like things were normal. "Nah. It was good though; weird to be allowed to drive around anywhere I wanted. You?"

"I didn't get laid either." Jake chuckled a little. "No chance. My time home sucked donkey balls, dude. The general was not too pleased with young

Jake. The parentals read me the riot act for failing half of my classes. They said I can't come home if this doesn't work out. I think they're bluffing, but I don't want to find out, you know? I mean, I've grown accustomed to a certain lifesty—"

"Did you tell them?" Nash interrupted him, irritated at his humor. Once again, that reckless feeling stirred inside of Nash. He guessed now was the time to confront Jake.

Jake didn't pretend like he didn't know what he was talking about. "Nope." When he saw Nash's shoulders slump, he hurriedly continued, "Why should I, man? Maynard doesn't know anything, and my parents were so fucking pissed about the grades. I was seriously nervous they were going to throw me out on my ass."

"Maynard's going to suspect something. He's going to wonder how your scores went from Fs to As and Bs, Jake." Nash threw his duffle bag to the ground and sat in his chair, annoyed that Jake hadn't come clean to his parents—or anyone else.

"Man! That guy has trust issues—it's a shame, really." Jake grinned at the irony of his observation.

Nash wasn't smiling back. "I don't want to have to tell anyone. I want you to do it, Jake." Nash said quietly. His heart was pounding in his ears, and he could feel sweat forming on his upper lip. He didn't know when he made the decision to turn him in if Jake didn't come clean. *Had he really made that decision?* Maybe it was never really a decision that needed to be made. Maybe Nash just needed to screw up the courage for this moment right now. He continued talking to Jake, his voice growing louder and more confident. "I want you to tell Maynard you cheated on the Chem GR." Nash couldn't believe he actually said it out loud. The last two weeks at home, all he wanted to do was call Jake and convince him to come clean. But he didn't because he was afraid Jake wouldn't be friends with him anymore. He was afraid Jake would tell Greene and Sully that Nash was a rat, and then Nash would lose them, too. Nash knew it could be social suicide to actually report someone—not just someone, but his very own roommate, his friend.

"Shit," Jake grunted, dropping down into his desk chair and oscillating back and forth, a fan with no air to blow.

"You know, I could go with you and you could come clean before it ever gets to an honor investigation. You're a Doolie—a freshman. They gotta know the pressure we're under. You can't be the first kid to cheat on a GR, Jake. It's gotta mean something that you would come clean. It's probably better to do it before Maynard gets suspicious about the grade." Nash continued to plead his case with Jake.

"Yeah." But Jake was still swinging back and forth, and he hadn't made eye contact with Nash. He was staring off into space. After a few quiet minutes, he spoke. "Maybe I didn't do so hot on the GR, so Maynard will never suspect."

"C'mon, Jake. The point isn't how well you did

on the damn GR. The point is that you cheated on the GR." Nash was getting angrier. "Do you really want to carry that with you for the next three-and-a-half years? That you cheated and didn't get caught? I know this shit matters to you."

"Don't get carried away, Nash. It doesn't matter to me *nearly* as much as it matters to you. I'm here because my dad expects me to be here. My dad was a fucking Rhodes Scholar his senior year, and I'm flunking everything. We're not the same. You're lucky your dad's not around to put that press—" Realizing his mistake, Jake abruptly stopped talking.

Nash felt like he had been punched in the gut, and all the air in the room had quickly been sucked out. The two sat in silence until Nash whispered, "That was a real dick move, Jake."

"I'm sorry, Nash. I didn't mean—" but Jake wasn't allowed to finish.

"Just shut up. I've heard enough from you." Nash sighed, exasperated with Jake. "You're flunking some classes, so what? So are about two hundred other Doolies. Shit, some of these people stay on academic probation all four years. Who the fuck cares? AcPro's not bad. It's mandatory study time, which you need anyway. We all graduate with the same commission." Nash's voice grew louder as he let out his anger.

"Dude! Why are you yelling? I feel like I'm back home with my parents," Jake pouted.

But Nash wouldn't stop. "I'm yelling because I'm pissed, Jake!" Nash began pacing back and forth as he continued, "There were like eight thousand kids who applied to this fucking place, and you and I were a couple of the lucky bastards they let in. We were invited into this history, this chance to join a legion of Air Force officers like your dad and *my* dad, you sonofabitch." Nash jabbed a finger toward Jake. "Yes, it sucks a lot of the time. Yes, it's the fucking hardest thing I've ever had to do. And by the way you're falling apart first semester, it's the hardest thing you've ever had to do, too.

But it's also awesome because we're doing shit that most of the country only dreams about doing. I'm meeting amazing people like Greene and Sully—and even you, dipshit. You're my friend, and I'm pissed because you're about to throw it all away by cheating on a stupid fucking test!" Nash finished and threw his hands up in the air as he plopped down on the neatly tucked bottom bunk.

The room was eerily quiet for what felt like five minutes, but was really only a few seconds. In those few seconds, Nash was convinced that he had made a mistake in unleashing all that on Jake. Their friendship had always been pretty light and fun. Jake would make jokes and Nash would laugh. Jake would struggle with an assignment or a quiz and Nash would help him study. Nash and Jake had never gotten into any arguments or even raised their voices at each other. Nash was certain he had gone too far, and now he would lose one of his best friends at the Academy. The rest of the year was definitely going to be awkward if this didn't work out. Nash prepared himself for an explosion as he slowly lifted his eyes to meet Jake's.

Instead, Jake simply picked up his backpack, turned around and walked out of their room without another word to Nash.

CHAPTER

17

Three days went by before Jake spoke to Nash again. During that time, Nash was determined not to break the silence. He thought it was important that Jake make the first move, whatever that would be.

In the mornings, Nash didn't make sure Jake was up, and they no longer exchanged sarcastic conversation with the other Doolies during their morning bathroom rituals. Jake didn't show up for his details during those three days either, but no one noticed except Sully and Greene. During chow, Jake sat at another table or ate at different times, leaving Nash to pretend like he didn't know what was going on when Sully and Greene asked him about it. By the third day, Nash was resigned that he had lost a friend. The rest of the year was going to suck even more now that he would have to go through it like this—trying to avoid his roommate who hated him.

Before lights out on the third day, Nash was just dozing off to sleep when he heard Jake quietly call his name. In fact, at first he thought he was dreaming it, so he didn't answer.

"Nash!" Jake repeated a little louder.

"Yeah?" Nash grunted, his voice thick from almost-sleep.

Then, silence. Jake didn't say anything for such a long time that Nash really did think he had dreamed it. He tried to quiet the pounding of his heart so he could hear him if he said it again. He had almost drifted off when Jake continued. "I can be a real ass sometimes."

Nash didn't move a muscle. He wasn't sure if he

was asleep or awake, and he didn't want to break whatever spell was cast.

"Did you hear me, Nash?" Jake questioned.

"Yeah, I heard you. Are you expecting an argument about that?"

"Fuck off," Jake chuckled. "I'm sorry I've been a dick. I'm going to tell Maynard."

"Why?" Nash asked.

There was another long silence, and then Jake sighed, "Because somebody told me it was the right thing to do. And fuck him because he's right."

Nash smiled in the darkness, before turning over to go to sleep.

After Jake talked to Maynard, the honor board convened quickly. It was barely a week later when Jake, Maynard, and Nash were called into the board to provide their official statements.

"Dr. Maynard, please tell us how you learned of

Cadet Nichols's alleged honor violation," the board president encouraged the chemistry professor.

"Cadet Nichols told me himself."

"Cadet Nichols reported the violation on himself?" The president raised an eyebrow.

"Yes, he did. Last Friday, Cadet Nichols and Cadet Kaplan entered my office and Cadet Nichols informed me he had made and used a cheat sheet for the Chemistry GR I assigned prior to the winter break."

"Had you suspected Cadet Nichols of cheating before he told you?" The board president asked.

"I hadn't graded the tests yet, so I didn't suspect anyone of anything. However, after the cadets left my office, I graded Cadet Nichols's GR. The grade alone would have raised my suspicions because he scored higher than eighty-five percent of the class."

"Thank you, Dr. Maynard. Cadet Kaplan, I understand you would like to make a character statement on behalf of Cadet Nichols?" The board president directed her attention to Nash.

"Yes, ma'am. Cadet Nichols owned up to his mistake—even before he knew if he would be caught. He's also a great roommate, always helping me finish my details, which might not seem like a big deal to the board, but it really is . . . " Nash thought he sounded like an idiot, but the board panel was so intimidating. He cleared his throat and continued, "Most importantly though, I trust him to do the right thing from here on out."

Nash looked over at Jake who was standing at attention waiting to answer questions from the board.

"Thank you, Cadet Kaplan and Dr. Maynard. Will you both step outside while we speak with Cadet Nichols?" The president waited for Nash and Maynard to leave the room, and for the heavy oak doors to swing shut behind them.

Twenty long minutes later, the doors opened, and Jake walked out with a little less pep in his step than normal. Nash said nothing, just fell in step beside him and they marched back to their dorm room.

Once safely inside, Nash couldn't take it anymore, "So!? What did they say?"

Jake threw himself down on his bunk, not caring about messing up the GI blanket with its perfect "E" fold. "I'm on honor probation for six months. If my math is right—which it probably isn't because I suck at math—that carries me through the end of the year, and into the beginning of next year! Plus, I have to write a letter of apology to Maynard. And I have to call my parents."

"That's awesome!" Nash forgot himself in his excitement that Jake wasn't being expelled.

"Shit, Nash, you have a warped idea of what makes something *awesome*." Jake began loosening his Air Force tie that was too tight around his neck. "They said that my instinct to cheat was not *acceptable*, but my decision to come clean was *redeemable*. They called me *redeemable*. Should I use that on the phone when I call my dad? He's going to lose his shit. Do you think it will impress him when I tell him they think I'm *redeemable*?" Jake smiled crookedly.

"You never know, dude. It just might. When are you going to call him?"

"I have two hours. Then I have to report back to the board when I've done it."

"Do you want me to hang out while you give him a call?"

"No, thanks. It's humiliating enough without your chipper ass in the background. Just get out of here. I don't need anyone watching me turn into a whipped puppy when my dad lays into me on the phone." Nash ignored Jake's bad mood, and almost skipped around the room. He was so relieved that his friend was going to stay.

"It'll be okay. Just do it quick, like ripping off a Band-Aid." Nash smiled.

"Easy for you to say, dickweed. You're not the one who has to make the call." Jake shot up quickly, almost hitting his head on the bottom of

Nash's bunk. "Hey! Why don't you call them and pretend to be me? Or maybe you could call them for me! You could really help me out—"

Nash shut the door on Jake's ideas, and headed for the bookstore.

"**M**y ass is beat, Nash. I can't lift my arms up high enough to brush my damn teeth!" Jake was complaining about his sore muscles. Part of his punishment was to march "watch tours" for three hours a day, carrying a cement-filled, rubber M-16 while dressed in his service dress. He had to march tours for five more months, three days a week. He was barely a month into his six-month punishment.

"That sucks, Jake. I really wish I could help, man. Truly." Nash grinned as he continued folding laundry on the floor of their dorm room. They were nearly back to their old ways.

"No you don't, asshole." Jake grinned. "I know you think I'm getting what I deserve, and you're right. But you're getting what you deserve too, because I'm going to breathe in your face every day for the next five months until I have the strength to brush my fucking teeth again."

Nash laughed at his ridiculousness. "It can't smell worse than the rest of you, you stinky bastard." It felt good to joke together—like his buddies back home.

"So I'm going to be living vicariously through you for the next couple of months until I can leave this shithole campus again. What are you doing this weekend?"

Nash knew Jake was throwing a pity party. The campus was beautiful at the Academy, and there was plenty of stuff to do. Arnold Hall hosted plays, comedians, and bands to entertain the cadets. Jake, Nash, Greene, and Sully had been hiking and horseback riding last weekend, and they didn't even have to leave base. There were trails and campsites all over the natural wildlife preserve that was the Air Force Academy campus.

"I think we're going to the movies tonight. Greene wants to see the new Matt Damon flick. You know the one where he's stuck on Mars?"

"Oh yeah! It looks decent. I can totally relate to Damon's struggle. Stuck far away from your friends as they return to normal lives . . . wishing someone would rescue you from the wasteland. I guess I'll catch it when it comes out on DVD," Jake joked, but Nash knew he was happy to still be at the Academy. Jake told Nash that his call with his dad went better than expected, and his dad actually told him he didn't give a shit about the boxing stuff if it was getting in the way of school. Jake seemed to be in much higher spirits, and working hard to improve his grades.

"So, how's Maynard been treating you?" Nash wondered if Jake was suffering through his class the same way he was before he brought the cheat sheet into the GR.

"You know what? He's not as awful as I thought. I've actually been learning some fucking chemistry when I have to report to him every day! Imagine that bullshit! And he's a lot easier to take one-on-one than in a room full of assholes who are raising their hands all the time, trying to prove how smart they are—he's not been a shit like I thought he was going to be after Waterbottle-gate 2015." Jake grinned again.

Nash went back to matching up socks and folding T-shirts. He thought about how Jake had turned himself in, and about how intimidating his dad was—but he came clean with him, too. Nash imagined how scared Jake probably was, but he did it anyway. He didn't know what the outcomes were going to be, but he did it anyway. Nash took a deep breath and spoke. "Okay. I want to say something to you, but I don't want you to turn into an asshole after I say it. Deal?" Nash actually felt nervous and couldn't look at Jake.

Jake quickly broke the serious mood. "No, I do

not want to go out with you, Nash. If you don't stop trying to date me, I'm going to turn you in for sexual harassment." Jake threw wadded socks at Nash's head.

"Don't flatter yourself. I just wanted to tell you that I think it's pretty cool that you didn't quit. You could have quit, and you didn't. I just wanted to tell you that."

Jake didn't say anything back to Nash, but Nash felt that he'd really heard him. Jake smiled.

Nash smiled back. "Did I ever tell you what I learned about my dad over the break? My mom gave me an award he earned that I never knew about, the Air Force Cross. And I've been doing some research on the Internet. I've learned some pretty cool things about the fighter squadron he belonged to . . . " Nash and Jake passed the afternoon folding laundry while he told Jake of the way his dad died fighting the enemy in Afghanistan.

Later that night, Nash, Greene, and Sully returned from the movies to seek out Jake in the dayroom.

"Sully, what did you think of the flick?" Jake asked.

"I thought it was very good, very very good. He was a very smart astronaut, don't you think, Greene?"

In all the ways that Suleyman was positive, Greene was realistic. "I don't know. I mean, how did he know all that stuff? He was a botanist, right? Since when do botanists know all that stuff about chemistry?"

"Maybe he went to the Academy," Nash joked.

"I'm serious," Greene turned her furrowed brow on Nash. "That guy was like a genius or something. I can't even figure out Chem two hundred, and he's growing potatoes in his own shit." Greene slumped down dejectedly on the dayroom couch.

"You're not afraid of Chem two hundred, Greenie!" Sully teased. "I think you're braver than that!"

Then Jake chimed in, "I think she's right. Some people just can't cut it, brain-wise, you know?" Jake jabbed an elbow at Nash. "If the difference between life or death depended on me knowing how to turn shit into potatoes, I guess I'm dead."

"He didn't have to turn shit into potatoes; he had to infuse the soil—"

Before Greene could set Jake straight on the intricacies of the plot, Nash interrupted. "Could we talk about something other than human shit, please?"

All four looked at each other and started laughing at the absurdity of the conversation. When the laughter died down, Greene spoke again, "Maybe the point of the movie was that we don't know what we're made of until we're tested." She gently nudged Jake with her shoulder.

"I know that's right," Jake grumbled.

"You're so right, Greene," Sully remarked. "When my family and I had to leave everything we had ever known to travel across the globe, I was terrified! I didn't want to leave my aunts and uncles back in the Sudan. I didn't want to leave my friends and my home. But now, I think how different my life would be if I hadn't left, if I had given up and refused to take one more step forward."

"Jesus, you win, Sully. You're more badass than all of us, okay? How am I supposed to feel sorry for myself when my friend is a fucking refugee?" Jake joked.

Sully laughed and looked down shyly. Nash threw his arm around Sully's shoulders and gave him a quick squeeze.

"I don't think I've been close to breaking yet," said Greene.

"Really? Not even when Smokey's breathing his fire down your neck, and we're doing push-ups until our arms can't hold us up anymore?" Nash reminded her. "How about when he's tossed your room for the fifth time that day—don't you just want to give up?"

"Nash! I thought you were using the o-face?" Jake chimed in.

"Dude. Not appropriate." Nash bladed his hand back and forth against his throat to indicate to Jake to keep his mouth shut on that topic. He wasn't sure if Sully and Greene would take Jake's crude jokes with the vibe intended.

"What is the o-face, Jake?" Sully asked.

"Nothing, forget it," Nash hurriedly said.

"Well, I guess I've probably come closer to reaching some 'breaking point' at the Academy than I have doing anything else," Greene agreed.

"I know that's right," Jake chuckled.

CHAPTER
19

The last three months of Doolie year went by in a strange alternative universe. The days felt like weeks and the weeks felt like days. It was some *Star Trek*-time warp shit, as far as Nash was concerned. It amazed him how much the Academy tried to pack into a twenty-four-hour period. Again, Nash thought they were purposefully overwhelming cadets to see who could take it and who would tap out. Just last week, another Doolie out-processed—the military's version of being disenrolled. It wasn't too common an occurrence anymore, now that they had made it through basic training, but it still happened occasionally. Nash no longer felt jealous of them when he heard about another one "biting the dust." He remembered what Captain Waters had said all those months back, "The Academy isn't for everyone." He had a greater understanding of what she meant by that now. The pace of the Academy, the demands of the place, were only for the truly mental. He guessed he would have to count himself among that group now—and Jake, too.

Jake kept powering through his punishment marches and extra instruction with Dr. Maynard. He even started joining Nash, Sully, and Greene every night for their study sessions. Even though he had to quit the boxing team, he seemed to be doing better in his classes. Jake told Nash he wasn't failing anything anymore. The biggest improvement was, of course, in Chemistry. Jake was even helping Nash, Sully, and Greene with Chem stuff during their study sessions. Yep, an alternate universe. And Nash was happy to see his Academy family surviving. They were a tight-knit group that had learned to push one another and support one another.

Now, end of year finals were kicking everyone's asses. Nash had slept a total of six hours in three days. Jake was hallucinating about hot girls in his sleep and making sex noises. During the day they were walking zombies chasing passing grades. In one day, Nash had a Calculus GR, a Chemistry GR, and two twenty-page essays due in English and Military History. Every day of finals was like the Bill Murray movie *Groundhog Day*. Everything was repeated in an endless loop of cramming for the finals of the day, writing a paper or two, surviving on Cheetos, Monster drinks, and gallons of coffee, and trying to get one or two hours of sleep in between. What made it tolerable was that everyone was in the same boat together. Everyone was trying to get through finals, and there was bonding and camaraderie in the misery.

The alarm went off, but Nash had been up for at

least two hours. He hurried to print off the last five pages of his paper on the Peloponnesian War, and kicked the bottom bunk to get Jake moving.

"Fuck you!" was the muffled response Nash heard over the beeping and buzzing coming out of the printer as it riffed off page after page. Nash took Jake's response as acknowledgement that he was, in fact, getting up.

"Last day, dude. A few more hours and Doolie year is in the books." Nash tried to encourage Jake to get his ass moving.

"Ugh! I hate everyone," Jake replied.

From down the hall, Nash could hear Greene's music blasting. She liked to play deep indie rock as a way to irritate the hell out of everyone to set the day off on the right foot. Some haunting voice was singing, "If you're still breathing you're the lucky ones. 'Cause most of us are breathing through corrupted lungs." *How fitting*, Nash thought. Only the Academy could make him feel like taking a boot up the ass was a fortunate thing.

"Let's go, Jake!" Nash shouted as he headed to the latrine for his morning routine. Jake threw his pillow at the doorframe in response, but Nash was already down the corridor. *Shit. Shower. Shave.* He might have to skip the shower this morning. He wanted to get that paper turned in before zero-seven to avoid the late penalty, and he still had to get his details finished so Smokey wouldn't have an excuse to beat his ass today. No push-ups, thank you very much, Smokey. Fuck you very much, as Jake would say.

As he spread the shaving cream across his stubble, his brain kept repeating: *Just a few more hours and then Doolie year would be over.* Nash tried to process it as he met his eyes in the mirror. He was almost done with his first year at the Academy. He stood frozen, caught in the moment of disbelief, until Jake came up beside him and broke the spell.

"Hey, dude. Are you fallin' in love with yourself, or what? Did you forget how to shave?"

Nash met Jake's eyes in the mirror next to him.

"Nope. Just thinking about shit," he said as he scraped his razor blade along his cheek. "Your parents here?"

There would be a Transition Parade, and Nash was so excited to see Mason and his mom afterwards. He couldn't believe his mom and brother were actually in town, but he hadn't been able to see them yet. He was even looking forward to the twenty-hour drive back to Indiana. Long roads, no upperclassmen, fast food, and no alarm clocks. That was Nash's plan for the next three days.

"Oh yeah, they're here. Probably to see if I really made it." Jake grinned at Nash before turning away and heading toward the shower stalls. "Get out of my way, fuckers! I'm in no mood today!" The rest of the guys threw towels and rolls of toilet paper at Jake, used to his bullshit antics—they gave as good as they got.

Sully pushed into the bathroom in time to see the mess everyone was making. He helped Nash start to pick up the rolls of toilet paper before they became wet wads of tissue.

Nash shouted above the noise of twenty-five guys in a six-sink latrine. "Don't make me bust your heads, monkeys. Clean this place up before I go crazy on your asses. You'll wish Smokey was here to save you!" Last month, Nash had been assigned the new detail of keeping the men's latrine in order. Nash couldn't believe he actually missed the days of carrying out trash at dawn.

Nash exited the bathroom and entered the noise of the hallway. Greene's music made its way past the throngs into his brain, *Muse* this time, breathing out the lyrics to "Madness." "I can't get these memories out of my mind and some kind of madness has started to evolve; I tried so hard to let you go but some kind of madness is swallowing me whole, yeah."

"Greene! Seriously?! Can't you play something else?" Nash hollered in her room's direction, knowing she was used to groans about her musical choices. He also knew she wouldn't give a shit to change it.

Nash hurried back to his room to staple together the final pages of his Military History paper, and his eyes caught on his blue book that must have fallen down from under his pillow where he stowed it every night. He had hoped that everything he needed to know would transfer by osmosis while he dreamed. So far, that hadn't worked. But he studied the damn thing so much, Nash felt like every word was burned into his brain. He picked up the book from the floor, and it flipped open to a well-worn crease in the pages: Roosevelt's quote. It was the longest quote the Doolies had to memorize, and it was one that Nash had been working on for weeks. He groaned at seeing it splayed across the page. Before he could fold the book shut, he took another look at the quote:

It is not the critic who counts; not the man who points out how the strong man stumbles, or where the doer of deeds could have done them better. The credit belongs to the man who is actually in the arena, whose face is marred by dust and sweat and blood; who strives valiantly; who errs, who comes short again and again, because there is no effort without error and shortcoming; but who does actually strive to do the deeds.

Nash felt Roosevelt was talking directly to him through his words on the page. As he continued to read about people who dared greatly and were willing to try for victory, even if it meant they could experience defeat, he recognized that was exactly why he needed to go to the Academy. Yes, he felt closer to his father here, and yes, he wanted to experience more than what Clarksville offered, but there was something else, too. Nash needed to be in the arena, no matter the outcome. His arena was the Academy. Maybe it was the lack of sleep, the overload in his brain, eating Doritos for breakfast, or the gallons of coffee coursing through his bloodstream, but he couldn't keep the smile from his face. He might be delirious, but he felt closer to euphoric. Standing in the doorframe of his room, surrounded by the noise of fifty other zombied Doolies, Nash felt good—really, really good.

Just then, Jake came from the bathroom and saw Nash standing in the doorway of their room. "Shake a leg, Kaplan! We got eight minutes to get to chow!"

Eight minutes? Nash thought. *Plenty of time.*